CONTENTS

THOSE

WHO

LIVED

FALLEN WORLD STORIES

MEGAN CREWE

Other Books by Megan Crewe

The Earth & Sky Trilogy

Earth & Sky

The Clouded Sky

A Sky Unbroken

The Fallen World Trilogy

The Way We Fall

The Lives We Lost

The Worlds We Make

Give Up the Ghost

Copyright © 2014 Megan Crewe

Illustrations by Ludi Price

All rights reserved.

ISBN-13: 978-1503111660

To the survivors,
every one of us

PREFACE

When I finished writing *The Worlds We Make*, the final book in the Fallen World trilogy, I knew that was the end of Kaelyn's story. There were some loose ends and questions left unanswered, but I felt her arc as a character was done and that exploring those avenues would drag the story on too long. I had some ideas about what happened after, and I figured readers would come up with their own, which was fine with me.

What I hadn't anticipated was seeing so many readers commenting on how much they wished I'd included more about later events and characters who hadn't been seen in some time. I still believed Kaelyn's story had ended where it should, but I couldn't help wondering, *What tales might I tell from the point of view of some of the other characters? What could happen in Tessa's version of the world, or Drew's, or Leo's?* And my writer brain immediately began spinning those stories.

It wasn't an ideal time for new inspiration. My husband and I had recently welcomed our first kid into the world, and it was difficult getting any writing at all done while looking after a three month old. On top of that, I had a new trilogy coming up that required I get drafting and editing other books. But the Fallen World story ideas kept gnawing at me. I wanted to give those characters' their voices, and I wanted to give something more to the readers I'm so appreciative of, who've followed the trilogy all the way through. Finally, with my agent's encouragement, I started outlining the stories and then, in a break between other drafts, wrote them out. I couldn't help liking them more and more as I worked on them.

Now I'm pleased to be sharing those stories with you. I'll note that my intended audience is readers who are already familiar with the trilogy, so you won't find a lot of recapping of past events, and as the stories all take place after the official end of the trilogy, the major developments in *The Worlds We Make* are thoroughly spoiled. If you haven't read that book or the previous ones yet and intend to, I recommend you start there.

You'll still find that not everything is wrapped up perfectly, mainly because I don't believe life ever does, and I try to reflect that in my writing. But you will get a further look into the friendly flu-devastated world from the perspectives of three characters whose heads you've never been inside before. I hope you enjoy reading them as much as I enjoyed the writing.

-Megan Crewe

Carry the Earth

CARRY THE EARTH

Meredith burst into the greenhouse with her thick, black hair flying wild and her hands waving like leaves about to break from a tree, and my first reaction was alarm. I straightened up over the patch of potatoes I'd been weeding, looking away from her to the wide glass walls. The rectangular shape of the log-built gathering house blocked my view of the fields beyond.

I didn't need to see the coming intruders to be prepared. As always, I'd kept my feet on the boards laid amid the plots of soil to avoid footprints and left a few scattered weeds so the other plants looked less cultivated. To add to the illusion that this former artists' colony was deserted, that there was nothing of value here, I'd need to stow my gardening gloves and trowel in the box concealed under the stone by the door. The bag of carrots I'd harvested I could bring with me to the cabin I shared with Meredith. I'd have to make sure none of her drawings were lying out before we squeezed into the compartment under the—

"Tessa!" Meredith said, grasping my wrist. I realized I'd tuned out at least ten seconds of chatter. Also, *she* didn't look alarmed. The opposite, actually. She was beaming. What I'd taken for panic at first glance must have been excitement.

I let my hands pause, the one still gloved dangling the glove I'd already removed. "I'm sorry," I said. "What's going on?"

"They're *back*," Meredith said, bobbing up and down. "Kaelyn, and Leo—they came back, just like she promised they would."

Not intruders arriving, but friends. Friends who, despite the promises made, we hadn't known would ever make it back. I found myself smiling too, with a rush of relief and surprise and a sensation that didn't quite fit, like the bottom of my stomach dropping out. Because I couldn't quite believe it? It didn't seem likely Meredith could be wrong.

"The car stopped at the side of the road," she was saying, "and Suzanne was about to sound the warning, but I just—I had this feeling, I said we should check with the binoculars and see what the people in the car did first—and then they got out, and I saw her, so I ran down—the snow's a lot thinner on the field now—and I

3

helped them carry—they brought a bunch of food—
Suzanne's just giving them some of the lunch."

As her voice raced along, she tugged me toward the
door, still carefully walking on the boards the way I'd
taught her. I stopped her long enough to tuck away my
gloves and trowel, because who was to say real intruders
couldn't show up today too? Then we padded together
across the slick layer of ice that coated the ground
between the buildings, to prevent footprints there.

The air outside the greenhouse was still a few
degrees below freezing. For a couple of days last week
it'd snuck above and turned the courtyard into a vast
muddy puddle before freezing again overnight. The
other colony residents had started discussing what new
strategy they'd switch to when spring arrived
completely. I might miss this: sliding one foot and then
the other across the smooth, solid surface of the ice. It
focused me.

They were back. Kaelyn and Leo. But not the others
—Gav and Tobias, and Justin, who'd run off after them?
There were a lot of things that could mean. Some good,
some bad. No use in speculating when we'd find out for
sure in a moment. Knowing at least the two of them
had survived was more than enough reason to keep
smiling when Meredith turned her blinding grin toward
me again.

*　*　*

It had been January when we first stumbled on the colony, when I'd decided to stay behind to help with the greenhouse and Kaelyn had asked if I would look after Meredith while the rest of them went on. Now it was March. Beyond that, I wasn't sure how many weeks had passed. A month-by-month calendar hung near the door to the kitchen, but I'd never seen much point in following it. The only plans I was making involved the gardening, and with that it was better to go by the signs in front of you, by sight or smell or touch, rather than relying on a generic timetable.

Meredith had been more stoic about the wait than I'd have expected from a seven-year-old with her cousin, the only family she had left, far away facing unknown dangers. The first week, she'd disappeared into our cabin and come out with tear-reddened eyes a couple of times. She'd never stopped peering toward the road whenever we crossed the courtyard. But whatever worries she'd had she'd kept to herself. I wondered now if she'd been watching the calendar, counting the days. Comparing them to the distances between here and Toronto and wherever else Kaelyn might have needed to go to find scientists who could replicate the vaccine. How much hope had she held on to?

I'd tried not to hope, or even really worry, other than a brief thought here or there. They would either come back, or they wouldn't. We couldn't know what was happening to them, what might delay them, until they were here again.

And now here they were.

When we stepped into the main room of the gathering house, Meredith darted from my side to the table where Kaelyn and Leo were sitting. Suzanne was seated across from them, talking in her low, even voice and the deft movements of her veiny hands. Kaelyn glanced past her to me, and Leo followed her gaze.

They were really *here*. Alive, okay. My throat choked up. Memories crashed over me, of so many things I hadn't thought about in months. The day Leo had first asked me out, by my locker at school, when there used to be school; the way he'd smile after we kissed, pleased and almost shy; the sputter of startled joy in his voice when he called me the second after the New York dance school called him with his acceptance, and I had, without any sense of the pending irony, thought, *This is probably the beginning of where we end.* Kaelyn at my door, the first friendly and healthy face I'd seen in a week, with a packet of seeds in her hand; the two of us exchanging conspiratorial grins before I'd unlocked one of the island summer homes with my dad's maintenance keys; the hollowness of her expression when I'd offered her a cup of tea, because it was all I could offer, after she came downstairs from one of her vigils after Meredith was infected.

The daze in Leo's eyes as he shook his head, when he'd returned to the island, and I'd asked him whether he'd seen my parents on the mainland. The pained curve of his mouth when I'd told him I was staying here and I expected him to move on.

People died, people parted ways. Even before the friendly flu, that was how it went.

But all of that was in the past, and here, now, Kaelyn was standing up, saying, "Hey, Tessa," her voice warm. They weren't exactly the same as when I'd last seen them: both thinner, Kaelyn's dark hair long enough that she'd pulled it back into a braid, Leo's olive-gold skin marred by a small scar beside his nose. Leo got up a little more hesitantly, I noticed. Maybe that pain wasn't all in the past for him.

"Almost everything in that stew we grew in the greenhouse," Meredith was saying, clutching Kaelyn's hand, "and I helped a lot."

I nodded in acknowledgement, walking the rest of the way over. "Hi," I said. There was so much that could be said that it overwhelmed me. "It's good to see you," I managed to add.

"Where's Gav?" Meredith demanded. "And Tobias? What happened in Toronto? You said you'd tell me when Tessa was here."

"I think I should leave you four to it," Suzanne said. She ambled over to the kitchen, and Kaelyn and Leo sat back down, Meredith squeezing in between them. So I sat down too, where Suzanne had been. Kaelyn looked at her hands, and Leo glanced at her as if offering to take this on for her. That was enough. I braced myself.

"The good news is," Kaelyn said, "my dad's vaccine is being produced. We had to go all the way to Atlanta, to the Centers for Disease Control, but there are still doctors working there, and they're making more. Along with—well, it's complicated. You know the people who were following us before, who wanted the vaccine?"

"The lady in the van," Meredith said with a grimace.

"Yeah," Kaelyn said. "They were working for a man named Michael, who's got a pretty big network across North America now. We were able to... negotiate a deal, where his people will coordinate with the CDC and help distribute the vaccine instead of fighting over it."

"Do you think he'll keep to that deal?" I asked. The people we'd encountered hadn't appeared to be particularly reasonable.

"So far he seems to be," Leo said. "There was a group, on our way back north, who confronted us—I think they were going to steal our supplies, but one of them recognized us and said Michael had sent out word not to mess with us, so they backed off. We don't know how long it'll take before the vaccine makes it up here, though. They hadn't produced enough to even cover all the survivors still in Atlanta when we left."

"But eventually…" I said.

"…no one should have to worry about catching the virus, at least," Kaelyn said, smiling for the first time. "Yeah."

It *was* good news, but in a way that didn't quite penetrate me. We were so isolated here that the friendly flu felt more like an occasional tragedy than a continuing threat. And Kaelyn had already given me a share of the vaccine before we'd left the island.

"So Gav stayed there?" Meredith said. "In Atlanta?"

Kaelyn's smile vanished as quickly as it had appeared. "No, Mere. He— You remember that man who ran at us when we were checking out that truck, who was sick, and Gav stopped him from getting close to the rest of us? It must have been because of him… Gav got sick. When we were in Toronto. There wasn't anything we could do." She paused, swallowing audibly. "Tobias too."

"But… I got better. You helped me get better, with that blood transfusion!" Meredith protested.

"Meredith," I said quietly.

"We didn't have any doctors, or medical equipment, or anyone to help," Kaelyn said. "I tried. Believe me." She gave a short laugh, so raw it hurt to hear it. Not just for me, it seemed, because Leo stepped in then.

"Justin's okay," he said. "*He* decided to stay in Atlanta, to keep an eye on things and pitch in where he could. We should let Hilary know, as soon as possible. Is she around?"

Meredith, abruptly on the opposite end of relating bad news, looked at me, as if I'd make her be the one to say it.

"Hilary passed on," I said. "A few weeks after you left, an infected woman wandered this way, and Hilary and a couple of the others ran into her in the woods unprepared. They were all exposed. The one guy, Kenneth, he ended up being okay, but Hilary got sick. And..." I spread my hands. They knew how it went. I hadn't even seen the three of them, other than Kenneth once it was clear he was fine, after they'd shut themselves away in the quarantine cabin. I'd only heard, through conversations passing by me, that Hilary had chosen to end her own life when she knew she was sick. When the other woman had become uncontrollable, the colony leaders had consulted with everyone and decided to "put her to sleep" to spare her further suffering. With the ground too frozen to allow a burial, the bodies had been wrapped up and placed a few miles into the forest.

"Oh," Kaelyn murmured. "She—she did know where Justin had gone, at least, didn't she? He said he wrote her a note."

"She knew he'd followed you. She knew you'd do your best to keep him safe. I think she understood. He'd been getting pretty restless here, she said." I didn't want to keep talking about the dead. "What are you going to do now?"

"Yeah," Meredith said. "Where are we going?"

Because of course they wouldn't stay here. And of course she'd go with them. I'd known that, but my stomach tightened as Kaelyn motioned vaguely.

"We're heading back to the island," she said. "I want to let everyone know we made it—and to see how they're doing. After that, I'm not sure."

"The roads are a lot better now," I said. "You'll have a faster trip than we did getting here."

"But you'll come too, right, Tessa?" Meredith said.

She had to ask. But I don't think Kaelyn or Leo was surprised when I said, "No. I have the greenhouse to look after here." And I had nothing there, really, to go back to.

Meredith dragged Kaelyn off to show her the few new things around the colony, and Leo came with me to gather Meredith's few possessions. They weren't even going to stay the night—Suzanne was concerned about them leaving the car parked nearby, and there wasn't anywhere safe to hide it.

"Meredith hasn't given you much trouble?" Leo asked as we mock-skated across the ice to the cabin. His dancer reflexes made me look as graceful as an elk in comparison.

"No, not at all," I said. "We were already pretty used to each other, since it was mostly just the two of us before, when Kaelyn was sick and her dad was working at the hospital all the time. And I think she thought being brave about it would somehow help Kaelyn get back."

"I guess it worked," Leo said with a rueful smile. "It really was a good thing she stayed here, and didn't— Some of the situations we got into, I don't know how we'd have managed to look after her."

"It was the right decision," I agreed.

The cabin was the same one Leo and I had shared the couple of nights after we'd first arrived here, though since they were all identical he might not have realized. The pencil crayons one of the artists had offered Meredith were neatly tucked into their box on the desk, but her sketches of tiered ball gowns and intricate necklaces littered its wooden surface. Some included notes about ideal types of fabric or alternate color schemes. I didn't know if she imagined people might still make and wear clothing like that in our lifetimes. It hadn't seemed like an appropriate thing to ask.

I retrieved her basket from under the bed, with a few changes of clothes the colony residents had found on their scavenging runs, a folded "book" with a short story one of them had written for her, and a drawing of a coyote she'd saved to show Kaelyn. Leo shuffled the sketches into a stack and set them inside, raising an eyebrow at the top ones. Wondering the same thing I did, I suspected.

"Can she keep these or are they on loan?" he said, picking up the box of pencil crayons.

"I'll get her to ask."

I looked around. Most of my things stayed in the greenhouse, so there wasn't much else in our small room. The empty chair and the bed that was going to be much more spacious with just me in it. Though I'd become pretty comfortable with sleeping leaned against the back wall so Meredith didn't bump me when she turned over.

"You know," Leo said, "Kaelyn would have encouraged you to come with us if she didn't figure you'd say you wanted to if you did. Not because she—or I—wouldn't want you along."

As he met my eyes, I couldn't see any hint of distress. Whatever pain I'd inadvertently caused him when I'd first declared I was staying here, it hadn't lingered, then. It wouldn't have been like Leo to hold a grudge, but all the same, my next breath came a little easier.

"I know," I said. "And she's right. I really am good here." Back on the island, all that waited was a vacant house, shattered glass around my little backyard greenhouse, burnt-out buildings, and a gravel pit full of corpses. I doubted even Kaelyn would want to stay long. I'd found a rhythm here. I knew what I could contribute, what was needed of me.

"I'm glad," Leo said with a crooked smile. "You *should* be someplace where you can feel that way. I know it's pretty hard to find these days."

His gaze drifted through the room again, dark eyes thoughtful beneath his smooth black hair, his mouth that used to always be wide with laughter pressing flat. Maybe I'd never expected us to last forever, but I'd been happy, being with him, while it lasted. I'd thought he'd be that sweet high school boyfriend you simply grow apart from and look back on fondly, not the guy you break up with in the middle of a global catastrophe because you needed different things to survive. He should have been off at dance school, wowing audiences and charming a girl who matched him.

Someone got the story wrong, I thought, amusement and sadness mixing.

He was going to walk out of here with that basket, and I was never going to see any of them again, Kaelyn or Meredith or him. It would be as though they'd never been here.

A jolt of urgency shot through me, the need to ground this moment and make it as real as I could. He knew where we stood; he knew this was a final good-bye, so he couldn't mistake what I was looking for. It couldn't hurt.

"Leo," I said, reaching to touch his cheek and draw him closer. His eyes jerked to me, startled. He stepped back just before my fingers grazed his skin. Taking my hand, he glanced down at it, and then back at me.

"I'm sorry," he said. "I should have told you. Kaelyn and I... we—"

I'd been wrong—it could hurt. "Oh," I said, cutting him off, my face warming. "*I'm* sorry. I shouldn't have assumed." I should have noticed. When they were sitting together, there must have been signs. Too busy thinking my own thoughts, Dad would have said with a bemused shake of his head. *I haven't got much else, these days*, I replied to his imaginary voice.

Leo was still trying to explain. "We'd known each other so long, before, and then, after Gav died, it just..."

"It's okay," I told him, because it was. "I'm not upset. I'm the one who broke up with you, remember? And I wasn't trying to suggest we get back together. Come on, let's bring this stuff to the car."

The icy breeze whipped inside when I opened the door, but there were no papers left on the desk for it to scatter.

All of this was okay. And anything that wasn't, I would make it be.

* * *

By evening, Kaelyn's news about the vaccine had spread from the few people she and Leo had talked to through the whole colony. Suzanne had taken on Hilary's leadership role after Hilary died, and throughout dinner people kept stopping by the table where she sat with the other two residents who were in their fifties, the three of them having a sort of authority in their greater experience. Partway through the meal, Suzanne stood up and called for everyone's attention.

"I can see we have a lot to talk about," she said. "Let's enjoy our food for now, and when we're finished eating, we'll have a proper discussion."

I stayed because I was already there, but once the dishes had been cleared and people started taking turns saying their piece, I was only paying half my attention. The questions brought up were ones even Kaelyn couldn't have answered, like when the vaccine would make it across the border and how we could find out when it did. My mind wandered back a few hours, to when I'd watched Kaelyn and Leo and Meredith cross the field back to the car—side-by-side, matching Meredith's shorter strides. They'd looked like a family. I'd felt out of place, waiting there, so I'd gone back to the greenhouse when they were only halfway to the road. But a feeling had crept up over me that Meredith had looked back when they got to the car to wave one last time, and had seen I was gone.

So it was only when Jon joined in that I realized the conversation around me had gotten a little more serious.

"The first threat has always been the flu," he said, his voice resonating through the room. Hilary had told me that Jon had come to the colony before the epidemic as a playwright, but he'd also been an actor. It was easy to tell. When he brought out his stage presence, he could make a request to pass the salt sound like some-thing Shakespeare had written. Even though he was one of the youngest residents, people listened to him.

"That should be our first priority," he went on from where he was standing by his table. "We're not safe here, and we know that. Is there anyone who wants to go through what we did with Hilary and April again?"

April—the woman who'd been infected along with Hilary—had been Suzanne's daughter. I'd have assumed Jon was playing to Suzanne, but the anguish that leaked into his voice wasn't an act. He and April had just begun seeing each other, or whatever you could call "dating" in a situation like this, before she'd been quarantined. Of course this mattered to him. But something about the way he said, *We're not safe here,* made me stiffen.

"We're safer here than just about anywhere else," Lauren said from across the room. "Kenneth and I saw what happened in the cities. You think there are fewer sick people wandering around somewhere like Ottawa?"

"You left Ottawa months ago," someone else piped up. "It'll be different now. Anyone who's still there must have been smart enough to avoid getting infected —anyone who wasn't will be *dead*."

"From what we've heard, the 'smart' people are nearly as dangerous as the friendly flu," another remarked.

"And it could be months longer before the vaccine gets up here," Kenneth put in. A few heads nodded at that. He'd faced the possibility of infection directly— that gave his opinion an extra weight.

"How long can we keep going here?" Jon said. "Our resources aren't infinite. We're better off making our own decision while we have a choice than waffling until we're backed into a corner."

My skin chilled as it completely sank in. This was about more than just how to get the vaccine to us, or who would arrange it. What they were really discussing was all of us *leaving*.

Suzanne raised her hand, and everyone fell silent.

"It's true," she said. "We may be forced to leave eventually. There will be a point when we have to travel too far to find supplies to justify the effort. Hiding our presence here is going to be much harder in just a couple weeks, once the snow's fully melted and more outsiders are on the move. That doesn't mean we should uproot ourselves now, but it is something to consider."

"So maybe we'll have to make do with less," Kenneth said. "At least here we can grow our own food all year round. It's not as if the grocery stores will be open next winter."

"We can grow plants indoors anywhere," Jon said. "All we need are windows."

"Since when are you a gardener?" Lauren said, and suddenly everyone was looking at me.

"What do you think, Tessa?" Kenneth asked. "How easily could we grow the amount of food we're producing here somewhere else—in a city?"

A moment ago I'd been watching the conversation from the sidelines. I hadn't been prepared to be yanked into the middle of it. "I, ah," I said, gathering my thoughts. And then my mind clamped shut with a hard certainty. I didn't *want* to be in the middle of this. I didn't want this conversation to be going on at all. I knew the greenhouse, I knew the tools I had here, I knew I could work with them. That was the job I'd agreed to.

"I don't know," I said. "The set-up we have here is meant to be used for this sort of agriculture. I can't say what it'd be like starting from scratch somewhere else not knowing what we'd be starting with."

"Well," Jon began. My hands clenched under the table. Before he could continue, Suzanne raised her arms again.

"We've only just gotten the news," she said. "We've barely had time to think *anything* through. There are resources in the book room we can consult. We all have our own areas of expertise, to whatever degree they may be useful." She, as a former painter, offered a slanted smile. "Consider the possibilities on your own and with each other, and we'll revisit this discussion in a few days."

I ruined a tomato the next morning. I was kneeling on the boards beside their plot, picking and pruning as I worked along the row of pots that kept their roots protected from any chill in the soil. Soon it'd be warm enough to transplant them, I was deciding. Then I reached and twisted off a small green globe without thinking.

I stared at it in my hand. It barely fit the hollow of my palm. The people on cooking duty could still cut it up and add it to something, but it could have grown at least three times as big. A waste. Why had I done that?

The door's hinges squeaked. I looked up, ready to direct Meredith to the beans, but it was Suzanne coming in. Because Meredith wasn't here anymore. This was the third time I'd forgotten that. Wherever my head was, I wanted it back.

"What needs doing today?" Suzanne asked, surveying the plots. She'd been coming by for an hour or two most days the last few weeks. To soak up the warmth she said, though she was pretty handy too.

"It's about time to open the vents," I told her. They dropped the temperature a little, but let out some of the humidity. A few of the plants had been going moldy before I'd arrived. "Then the bean seedlings are ready to go in."

The vents creaked overhead. Suzanne padded over to the plot I'd worked over a couple of days ago in anticipation of the planting. "We'll be able to grow even more once it warms up, I suppose?" she said.

"We'll have more options," I said. "And we could grow some things outside too. We'll have to be careful about the heat in here in the summer."

She made a humming sound, and I wondered if she thought we'd still be here in the summer. I turned back to the tomatoes. Grip. Twist. Pinch. The ripe ones formed a solid weight in my hands, the warmth of the sun in their smooth skin. Sometimes the loamy green smell of the air in here, so different from the cold prickle of pine outside, filled me up like a sort of drug. I'd look down at a plot I'd just started on and find myself at the end. Meredith would say she'd called my name a couple of times and I hadn't answered. "What were you thinking about?" she'd ask, and I couldn't remember. Maybe nothing. Maybe I'd just been floating along, existing only in the work.

I wanted to sink into that zone now, but I was too aware of the rustle of Suzanne's clothes. The tap of the seedling trays against the boards. The sigh of her breath.

"I hope you didn't feel cornered last night," she said after a while.

"It's all right," I said.

"We do value your opinion. You've been a great help already."

"I like working with plants," I said with a shrug.

"You did a lot of this, before?"

"I wanted to do it for my whole life," I said. "Develop new, more diverse varieties of common crops. Help farms increase sustainability." There weren't enough people left now for diverse plant genetics or overworked land to really be a problem, of course.

"Well, for someone as young as you are, you certainly have yourself together," Suzanne said. "Be proud of that, all right?"

We know you've got yourself together, Dad said, the last time we spoke on the phone. *Just hold on without us a little longer, all right?*

That had been months and months ago. I'd seen the phone he must have been speaking into in the harbor office, when Tobias had brought the bunch of us across the strait from the island after his soldier colleagues had dropped their missiles on the town. Someone had left the dead receiver off the hook in the empty room that smelled like stale potato chips.

"If you ever—" Suzanne started, her voice like a burr prickling against my skin. I stood up.

"Terrance said they found some fertilizer on that last scavenging run," I said. "I should go see where they've put it."

I didn't realize I'd left behind the basket of tomatoes I'd filled until I was halfway across the courtyard.

Jon caught me just as I came out of the bathing area entrance after my evening shower. I'd taken only a couple of steps away from the gathering house toward my cabin when he said my name. He was standing at the edge of the courtyard in the declining light, his hands tucked casually into the pockets of his wool coat. His head cocked to the side, bare except for his dark brown curls. He smiled when our eyes met, a little smile that acknowledged the potential awkwardness of the situation while promising he meant well, and I knew what he wanted to talk about.

But there wasn't anything I could do to prevent it, so I stopped and watched him walking over. He had a distinct way of moving, more studied than Leo but still graceful. A classically attractive face: high cheekbones, straight nose, strong jaw. He looked a lot like I'd imagined my college boyfriend might look like, when college was a thing in my future, which I'd found almost funny when it had first occurred to me weeks ago but now was only annoying.

"What?" I said, a little of that annoyance bleeding out. I hadn't meant it to. But my hair was damp—the two women who'd come into the changing room had kept looking at me while they chatted, and I'd left without drying it completely—and the air was cold enough that my breath frosted in it. I hadn't thought I'd need a hat for this short walk.

Jon didn't meander around the subject, at least. His little smile disappeared, and he said, "I haven't changed my mind. I believe what I said yesterday. Suzanne respects you. If you said we could manage, away from here, she'd listen."

"Why would I say that?" I asked.

"It's true, isn't it?" he said, frowning. "A greenhouse in The Middle of Nowhere, New Brunswick, doesn't have magical properties a greenhouse in Montreal or Ottawa or Toronto won't. And in a city we'd be able to scavenge everything we needed while we settled in."

"You don't know what we'll find," I said, and added, honestly, "I haven't given it much thought."

"You're already protected," he said. "But don't you care at all what happens to the rest of us?"

"Why should my opinion matter more than anyone else's?" I said. It wasn't as if I was even really part of the community. They had a history with this place and with each other in their shared artistic interests, and I'd been fine with that. "If you want to go, you should go. And whoever else wants to, too. Whoever wants to stay can stay. Why do you have to turn it into a fight?"

He was silent for a moment, tucking his chin behind the collar of his coat. His eyes, studying me, were very dark. I couldn't make out what color they were in this light—couldn't remember if I'd ever taken note before.

"We're stronger together," he said. "We *need* each other. We need the skills everyone brings to the table— skills like yours. That's worth fighting for. I'm trying to make sure we don't break what we've already managed to construct."

There was a poetic elegance to those last words, as if, if he explained it prettily enough, it would change what he was actually doing.

"This isn't a play," I said. "Things are going to break whatever we do. You can't just script us into a happy ending. Good night."

I left the light off inside my cabin, shedding my coat and crawling onto the bed. When I closed my eyes, his were still looking at me, dark and expectant, until I finally drifted to sleep.

* * *

Whenever I walked into the gathering hall's main room for a meal, people were talking about it. In the shower rooms, too, and outside when there were tasks to help with in the courtyard. I didn't join the conversations, but voices were raised often enough that I heard plenty. Another scavenging run went out, on the two snowmobiles kept hidden in the woods, and when they returned with sleds full, everyone had an opinion about how long the trip had taken and how much had been found. The haul didn't look especially different from the last several runs to me.

Meredith had always been curious about the colony residents, so when she'd been with me, we'd usually taken a table with a couple of others and I'd mostly listened while they talked. I'd liked sitting with Hilary the most—she'd had an enthusiasm for food that complimented mine for the garden, and sharing bits of my ideas had ended up happening naturally. But then, after she'd gotten sick…

When I could, I ate alone in the midst of the commotion. When Kaelyn had delivered the news that the vaccine worked, she must have imagined it would be a relief. But people seemed *more* worried than before, even though nothing here had changed.

Three days after Kaelyn and Leo had come by, Lauren was working in the kitchen when I dropped off the greenhouse harvest. She looked over the contents of my basket with the perpetually mournful look created by those deep-set eyes in that narrow face.

"The white beans should start coming in a few weeks," I said. "Extra protein."

She nodded, and then peered at me as if she'd just remembered who I was.

"A few weeks," she repeated. Her fingers gripped the edges of the basket, so tight her knuckles whitened. "You're not going to leave, are you?"

"What?" I said.

"With Jon and them," she said, low and urgent. "You know if they go they'll want you to come. But we need you here if we're going to manage. Please."

I stared at her, speechless. "I wasn't planning on going anywhere," I said finally.

"Good," she said. "Good." She reached out as if to pat my arm, and I edged backward with a vision of her squeezing me the way she had the basket.

That night in the gathering house, an argument between two tables broke into outright yelling. Suzanne banged on her tabletop and got up. The whole room, those arguing and those who'd been watching, fell silent.

"I think we've had enough of that," Suzanne said. "You've all had time to think and research and talk. Tomorrow after dinner, anyone who wants to suggest a plan of action can get up and present it, *uninterrupted*, covering all the points they feel they need to. And when everyone who wants to has spoken, we'll take a vote. Until then, please try to remember that we're a community, and we all want what's best even if we disagree on what that is."

When she sat back down, everyone around me returned to their food and their quieter conversations. My gaze skimmed the room, my fork hovering over my half-finished pasta. I'd been hearing a lot, the last few days, but I hadn't been keeping track of who'd been saying what. Who was for the whole "community" picking up and leaving, and who was for us all staying here? Who might be in the middle, thinking the group should split apart?

I had no idea how the vote would go. But no matter what Jon had said, tomorrow something was going to be broken.

I was checking the bean plants the next day when it occurred to me that maybe none of what I was doing in that moment mattered. Maybe tonight everyone would decide to go. While I supposed we could bring along a few seedlings, we were hardly going to carry the contents of the greenhouse with us.

"You all right, Tessa?"

Suzanne's voice tugged me back to the present. I was crouched there, my hands dug into the soil. I had the urge to take off my gloves so I could feel exactly how warm or cool it was, rub the soft grains between my fingers. But I wasn't sure how long I'd already been hunched there unmoving, for her to have asked that.

"Yeah," I said, getting up and brushing my hands together. "Just thinking."

She was pouring water into the channels between the plots, using the buckets I'd filled with snow yesterday and brought inside to melt overnight. If we wanted to avoid using up well water on the plants, we were going to need to find some large trough-like containers to catch rain once the snow was gone.

If we were still here.

I knelt by the lettuce patch to inspect the leaves for bugs. There weren't many this time of year, but all the major tasks were taken care of. Now that I'd gotten the foundations in place, I could probably write up a daily to-do list and the colony residents could handle everything here on their own. Until summer. It'd get tricky again then, but that was months away.

"You don't talk much about your folks back home," Suzanne remarked. She paused, twisting a strand of gray-blond hair back into the clip that held it away from her face. Not bothering to look over, as if it wasn't a weighted comment.

"I don't have 'folks' back home anymore," I said. *Crunch*, a beetle shell under my thumb. "So there isn't much to talk about."

She drew in a breath. "You know, when April... When we had to let her go, I couldn't quite accept it at first. You never think, especially after you've seen them grow up, that you're going to outlive your kids. But it was harder that way. Holding myself back from the full blow. It just hangs over you, waiting."

"I accept it," I said. *Crunch. Crunch.* I ripped the edge of a leaf. "I accepted it before I even knew for sure."

Did she think it was the same? She'd seen April's body, helped them carry it into the woods, and said a final good-bye. I'd gotten silence from the phone and an empty room. But I'd known. I *knew.*

"I just wonder, the way you keep to yourself, if you've given yourself a proper chance to settle in..."

I was on my feet, spinning toward her in the same motion, before I felt the flare of anger inside me. "I'm here," I snapped. "I wouldn't *be* here if I thought there was any chance they were out there for me to find. Why can't this just be the way I am?"

She was looking at me now, hurt and concerned. My skin crawled at the thought of the reassuring words she might try to offer next. I jerked off my gloves.

"I'm going to get some fresh air," I said before she could speak, and went out.

It wasn't just fresh air I needed, I thought, standing

behind my cabin and gazing into the stretch of pines. A fresh space. A fresh atmosphere. Suzanne hadn't done anything wrong, really. I was just getting wound up by all the debating. My head was too cluttered.

While everyone was eating lunch, I went to one of the cabins that held our supplies. I took a tent, a few blankets, a box of granola bars, a jar of peanuts, and a backpack. I didn't need much. Just to leave, let my mind clear, and return after they'd decided. Maybe it'd all be back to usual. Or maybe I'd walk up to the cabins and find them cleaned out.

A chill passed through me at the image. But it didn't make much difference, did it? The things that mattered to me would still be here.

I waited to leave until it was getting dark, around dinner time. Jon passed me on his way to the gathering house as I left the greenhouse with a ripe tomato in my coat pocket. He nodded in greeting and said, "You'll be coming?"

To dinner, he meant. Which meant, to the vote. "In a minute," I said.

When the last few residents had headed in, I hefted the backpack over my shoulders and set off.

There were patches of bare earth amid the snow that ringed the bases of the trees. I walked on them as much as possible, to avoid leaching away the warmth in my boots. The evening air was crisp but not sharp in my throat. I found a comfortable rhythm, stretching my legs with long strides, pushing off the ground I crossed and left behind.

I judged it'd been about an hour when I reached a small clearing, the yellow grass dusted with frost. It was completely dark now. Stars glittered in the circle of inky sky that was framed by the treetops. *Here*, I thought.

Before I set up the tent, I followed the edge of the clearing the entire way around, peering into the forest in all directions. I spotted no sign of anyone living nearby. At the opposite end of the clearing, a small river ran past, its banks snow crusted and its surface solid with rippled ice. I broke away a small chunk—it wasn't very thick—and brought the water beneath to my mouth with my cupped hands. The cold stung my fingers and my throat and seemed to trickle right down to my toes. It fixed me to the snowy ground.

I was here. Just me. The comments, questions, looks, and everything else that had been heaped on me in the colony over the last few days sloughed from my skin like autumn leaves.

After a couple of mistakes, I got the tent up. I unfurled one of the blankets outside it and lay down in the middle of the clearing, staring at the stars. There were so many I lost track when I tried to count them. I held up my arm and watched them being blotted out by my hand. Still there, just unseen.

The ground beneath my back was firm. Stretching out on all sides, all the way around the planet. For a second, the thought of the vastness of it took my breath away. I was held by it, by the world and its pull.

Somewhere out in the darkness Hilary and April's bodies had been laid to rest. To return to the earth. Maybe the idea should have been unnerving, but it comforted me. If every one of us returned eventually, then no one was ever really lost. I had wandered off into the woods without a map or a clear destination, but I knew exactly where I was. I was in the shape of my hand against the stars and the hard surface pressing against my back.

If only I could just stay here.

In the morning I woke up bundled amid the blankets in the tent. I had a pain in my shoulder from lying on that hard ground and an ache in my stomach. Without shedding the blankets, I sat up and dug the box of granola bars out of the backpack. I ate a couple, and the last handful of peanuts, but the ache didn't leave, only twisted into a mild queasiness. The food felt gritty in my throat. I was too used to hot oatmeal and pancakes from the colony's kitchen.

I'd have to get over that.

The decision would be made now. The arguments

presented and the votes cast, far from my spot in the woods. I tried to push the thought away, back to that other place. I got up, stretched my legs with a walk around the clearing, and scooped a drink from the river, but it stayed with me. An uncertainty, hanging over me. Waiting, the way Suzanne had said, although she'd been talking about grief.

Just beyond the ring of pines stood a birch with icicles dangling in a jagged line down its branches. A bird or a squirrel or some other animal—Kaelyn might have been able to tell—must have scampered along one of those branches and jostled some free. Splinters of ice littered the shallow snow around its trunk. A slice of sunlight glinted off them.

In my former backyard, on the island, shards from the smashed walls of my first greenhouse were probably still scattered in the snow, if the snow on the island hadn't already melted, leaving the glass to mingle with mud and grass. The footprints of the boys who'd destroyed it would be long washed away. Their lives, the walls my dad helped build, the studies I'd started in cross-pollinating different strains of vegetables, my mom's hands on my shoulders as she told me I was going to do great things for the world. The world she'd been talking about. Most of the things I'd planned to do, the future I'd pictured—the friendly flu had washed all that away too. Like an immense flood only the strong, the lucky, and the stubborn had withstood.

I wasn't sure which of those I was anymore.

I'd seen the colony's greenhouse and flung myself at it wide-armed, but maybe that had been foolish. Foolish to think I could replace even one piece of what I'd lost. That there was anything I could hold onto that wouldn't be broken too.

That greenhouse was still there, of course. Even if everyone else left, they couldn't stop me from staying. I could keep to myself there and tend to the garden, the same as always. I saw it like a premonition: myself, red hair strung with as much gray as Suzanne's blonde, a wandering benefactor. Walking the roads with a bundle of seeds and roots to pass on to whomever could use them, looping around in my journey to return to where I'd started from.

My eyes misted up, a tear tracing a prickling line down my cheek before I'd realized I was crying. What was there to be upset about? I could have what I wanted. The garden, the work, and peace.

Unless that wasn't what would make me happy after all. I groped inside for a sense of it, of what I wanted— not just could tolerate or accept but actively *wanted*.

Nothing, I came out with. *I don't want anything.*

That couldn't be right. But no other answer offered itself up.

*   *   *

I hadn't meant to be gone for very long—and my queasiness had already circled back around to hunger with only two granola bars left in the box. I took down the tent, the poles rattling together and the fabric warbling against itself, stuffed it into the backpack with the blankets, picked up the pack... and set it back down.

I'd thought coming out here by myself would clear my head. It had seemed to last night. But now my mind was cluttered with uneasy thoughts again. I couldn't blame anyone but myself.

It should have been simple. Go back, get to work in the greenhouse, let the others do whatever they were going to do. So why did it feel so hard?

I left the pack and went down to the river. The water was still sharp on my tongue. I looked out across the span of ice, seven or eight feet wide, stretching into the woods in both directions. Dark patches mottled the white-gray surface where the water threatened to break through.

That was more like the truth than the ground I was crouched on. A thin solid layer suspended over a current that could wash it all away at a hike in the temperature or the crash of a fallen tree.

I straightened up and edged over from my drinking hole. Carefully, I set one foot on the ice. Then the other. The ice held, emitting a soft creaking like the wind through the greenhouse vents as I eased toward the middle. I spread my feet apart and stood there, gazing down the line of the river. The trees along its bank bent toward it, forming a ragged sort of tunnel. The dark patches blended into the shadows they cast.

This is it, I thought. *This is where I am. So where do I want to be?*

A breeze tickled under my hair, across my neck. I left my scarf loose around my shoulders. I had no idea how deep the water just an inch or two beneath my feet might be. My attention drifted down to the shifting current, followed it along the curves and bends of the river—and came back empty. There was still just me, alone in the woods, adrift without being in motion.

Alone. The ice creaked louder, with a crackling edge, and that one notion overwhelmed the rest. I could fall through and no one would see. No reaching hands would grasp mine and pull me out.

Panic fluttered in my chest. I took a hasty step and a seam parted in the ice to the right of my boot. Water seeped up through it. I stiffened. With a tentative slide of my other foot, I eased away from the crack. The treads of my boots scraped over the uneven surface, one and then the other, like I'd done between the colony buildings for the last two months.

My heel crunched through the ice by the bank, forming a geometric pool. I scrambled into the drift of snow, onto the firm ground, my heart thudding. As I glanced back the way I'd come, I gripped the low branch of a nearby tree, as if the river might try to pull me back.

The crack looked like little more than a sliver from here. Not so threatening. I drew in a breath and released it. I'd been fine.

Then I turned around and saw Suzanne in the clearing by my pack. Beneath the line of her woolen hat, her eyes were wide and worried. She took a couple of steps toward me.

"I didn't want to startle you," she said. "You looked like... I'm so glad you got off the ice."

"Of course," I said, confused by her intensity. "I wasn't going to stand there forever."

"No," she agreed. "I was afraid maybe you wanted it to break."

That I— Oh. The thought of plunging into that frigid water sent a shudder through me. "I don't want to *die*," I said with a little laugh.

But the way she was still studying my face, maybe that wasn't obvious. I imagined what the scene must have looked like from her point of view. Remembered how I'd felt poised over the river and standing in the clearing just a little while ago.

Nothing.

I didn't want to die, no. But how much was I alive? I was here, substantial enough to touch the earth, to blot out stars, but a rock could do that. Life put down roots and extended leaves. When was the last time I'd felt I could do that?

Maybe a part of me was already dead. Maybe it had died like my parents, silent and unseen, and that was why I hadn't noticed. Until I'd come to myself and looked inside and found nothing but a vacant space and a disconnected line.

All at once, the sensation of aloneness that had struck me on the ice pressed in twice as hard.

"Oh, hun," Suzanne said, taking another step forward. She opened her arms, and even though something inside me still balked, I *wanted* so much I didn't care that she wasn't Mom or Dad or that I barely knew her. I knew she wanted to be there for me.

I stumbled to her and she wrapped me up, my face pressed against the padded down of her coat, damp with the tears already leaking out. She held me and rocked us gently on our feet. A low anguished sound came out of my throat. Suzanne didn't say anything, just hugged me tighter.

I sobbed and sniffled, and one clear thought floated above the rest. I wanted her to understand.

"They're never coming back," I said. I'd known that. I'd thought that. I was sure I'd even said it, to Leo, or to Kaelyn. But saying it now, the truth of it filled me as if I was only just uncovering it. They were gone, and I'd never even had a chance to save them. My parents and so many others, lives upon lives across the entire Earth. And even the living didn't always come back.

"No, they're not," Suzanne said softly. "But they never completely leave either. We carry them with us. It does help, but I know it hurts too."

Yes. I had been carrying them, tight and close around me like an impenetrable casing. But I was here, alive, inside the squeeze of Suzanne's embrace. I caught my breath. The crying had left salt in my mouth.

I stepped back, but not so far that Suzanne couldn't keep one hand on my arm. "How did you know where I was?" I asked.

"You left enough footprints to follow," she said. "I would have gone after you last night, when we noticed you hadn't come to dinner—Jon was worried; he said he'd seen you right before and you'd looked a bit odd—but I thought you might need some time on your own. I didn't want you to feel that we didn't care whether or not you came back, though."

So Jon had been thinking about more than just campaigning for votes. "How did it go?" I said, my stomach clenching. "What did everyone decide?"

Suzanne's expression turned puzzled. Then her eyebrows rose. "We didn't have the debate or the vote, Tessa. Everyone felt you should be a part of it too."

"Oh," I said. So the question was still looming. The

clenching inside me became a knot. "I don't know what's the best thing to do."

"None of us knows," Suzanne said. "We'll just make the best guess we can. And the things you know, about growing food, about the people we might have to deal with outside the colony, they'll help us do that. If you're willing to talk about it with us."

About trying to find another, useable greenhouse in a city, or ways to garden without one. About the stories Kaelyn and Leo had related, about this Michael, his Wardens, and the other survivors.

It wasn't as if the question would go away because I pretended not to see it. Jon had turned to me, and Lauren too, because they'd wanted to include me. Because what I told them could make a difference in whether all of us lived or died. I was already a part of it —part of the colony, part of the community—whether I liked it or not.

Right then, with the gentle contact of Suzanne's hand by my elbow, that knowledge didn't feel like a demand. It felt like a welcome. These people weren't gone. This time I had a chance.

"I can do that," I said. "I'll be there."

Trial by Fire

TRIAL BY FIRE

"Hey, Drew, Michael wants to see you."

A statement like that made everyone in the workshop glance over. Quickly, a side-eye toward me and then back to their jobs. When Michael called for someone, it was either very good news or very bad. Everyone was curious which... and no one wanted to be implicated in the latter.

I pushed my stool back from the table, set down the circuit board of the radio transceiver I'd been augmenting, and headed for the doorway where the guy who'd passed on the word was waiting. As soon as I stepped into the hall, he ambled off. It wasn't as if I needed further directions. Michael always held audience in the same place.

On my way to the former police training center's gymnasium, I considered the possibilities. Most of the last few days I'd spent either in the tech workshop or the communications room. I didn't remember noting down any especially exciting or disturbing information from my scans of the airwaves. I'd relayed a few reports from Wardens in other states about skirmishes won and supplies plundered, and passed on orders as instructed. It could be I'd fumbled a detail that had thrown a wrench in one of Michael's plans, but that would be a first. I'd achieved the role of lead radio operator through a precision I wasn't cocky enough to let slide.

Well, I told myself as I pushed past the double doors into the long, high-ceilinged room that smelled faintly of old sweat, *maybe he just wants to thank you personally for all your hard work.* Sure. I'd feel more comfortable believing that if my bottom left molar didn't still ache when I chewed, a memento of the punch Kaelyn's friend Justin had given me a month ago —on my request, so I could cover my involvement in their escape from the jail cells downstairs.

But that *had* been a whole month ago. The Native guy who was one of Michael's primary "field officers" here, Chay, had questioned me about it, and then Michael himself, and they hadn't appeared to have trouble believing that the skinny queer boy who seemed happiest dissecting the innards of whatever electronic device you set in front of him might have been overwhelmed with concern for a prisoner faking injury, unlocked a cell without thinking, and gotten himself clocked and the keys stolen. The watery gas in the cars in the lot had been blamed, as I'd intended, on the crack in the storage container's lid and the previous day's rain. I'd been chewed out, which I could tolerate, been taken off the security rotation, which I didn't mind, and been assigned to help Martha, one of the mechanics, fix Nathan's pet Mercedes, which had been less than fun but survivable. Otherwise, for the last few weeks I'd been left to my regular duties. No doubt it helped that, from the impressions I'd gotten, Michael was happier with the vaccine arrangement my little sister had concocted after her escape than he'd been while he had her imprisoned.

But you never knew, with Michael. I found myself wondering, as the tapping of my sneakers against the varnished floor echoed down the length of the gym, whether I should have already risked trying to reach out to Kaelyn again. Whether I should have kissed Zack longer before he went back to his room last night. If this went badly, there were things I'd have liked to have known, things I'd have liked to have said.

Well, it was too late for that now. I'd just have to contrive a way through this like I had with everything else life had thrown at me so far.

Michael was poised in his usual spot behind the immense executive desk he'd had hauled down from one of the offices upstairs. Two guards with rifles stood by the far corners of the room behind him. He was typing on the laptop I'd gotten working for him—worth the electricity for the time it saved him in processing, he'd said, and I guessed it would be tricky keeping track of pods of allies, supply stockpiles, and vaccine deliveries and payments across an entire continent with just your head and a pen and paper.

At the sound of my footsteps, he looked up. No hint of satisfaction or frustration in his expression. He shut the laptop and leaned his elbows onto the desk as he watched me approach.

I always forgot just how penetrating his gaze was until it was fixed on me again.

"Drew," he said as I stopped at the red line on the floor, five feet from the desk. His tone was good-humored and dry, as if he knew a joke he wasn't planning on sharing. "Prompt as always."

"I figured if you wanted to see me an hour from now, you'd have called for me an hour from now," I said.

His mouth stretched with a slow smile, but it didn't have much warmth in it. "If only all the people I deal with had that much sense."

Anyone who delayed responding to a summons from Michael I suspected was suffering more from fear than a lack of sense, but it didn't seem very sensible to bring that up.

"Let's get straight to the matter at hand." Michael glanced at his guards with a dismissive gesture. "Take a break—swing back around in ten minutes."

My stomach sank as they bobbed their heads and ducked out the side door without comment. What was it he didn't want them to witness?

"This arrangement with the CDC," Michael went on, and I jerked my attention back to him. "It's been running smoothly long enough that we're going to increase production. I'd like to see some of the vaccine make it up to Canada—I didn't leave my home country to abandon it. Because the distance requires our communications be second-hand, I want someone up there who's completely familiar with the arrangement to manage distribution and collection. So I'm sending Nathan."

"What?" I couldn't help blurting out. Nathan, who shot off his mouth at every opportunity, who criticized every decision Michael made... Ah. Maybe there was a sort of logic to relocating him hundreds of miles away. Everyone had been watching to see how their clash would play out. Nate was mouthy, but he also ferreted out other survivors and their hoards of provisions—and dispatched any of the former who objected to the Wardens taking the latter—with a ruthless efficiency that you had to recognize got the job done even if you didn't like how he did it. Kicked out, he'd be even more of a thorn in Michael's side, and executing a useful tool simply to stop his back talk would look like weakness. Still, letting Nathan that far off the leash seemed like an enormous risk all on its own.

"Good," Michael said to my startled exclamation. "You obviously understand there are reasons for concern. And that's why I'm sending *you* as his second in command."

"*What?*" I said again, stupidly, but it was either that or let my jaw hang slack.

"I need someone with sense keeping an eye on him," Michael said. "Keeping him in line, if need be. Are you going to tell me you're not up to the job?"

There was a warning in his voice now. I clenched my teeth. Michael might have forgiven my "mistake" with the prisoners, but Nathan had shoved me around a couple times in the week afterward, pissed off that he'd been, in his mind, so close to getting Kaelyn and the others to give up the vaccine and let him prove that his methods—torture and physical intimidation, mainly— trumped the psychological approach Michael had started with. He'd been just shy of adding to the bruises Justin had left on my face before a few of the other guys had stepped in, not so much because they liked me as because they hated him. And now Michael wanted me to work directly under the guy while also getting in his way if he went too far? Maybe Michael hadn't forgiven me after all. This sounded like a suicide mission.

"Are you asking me to do it or telling me?" I said carefully.

"There's always a choice," Michael said. "But I think you'll want to do it for yourself, not just for me."

"Why's that?"

He steepled his fingers. "There are people you know up there," he said evenly. "You're familiar with the crew in Toronto. And I'd imagine you'd like to be on hand in case Nathan happens to cross paths with your sister again."

His inflection hadn't changed. He just held my gaze steadily. He knew? How long had he known? Or maybe this was a feint.

"My sister?" I ventured.

"The CDC finally delivered the copies of some records I asked to see," he said, tapping a folder off to the side of the desk. Just shy of the revolver he always kept there. "They confirmed my speculations. I already knew Kaelyn had the vaccine because of her father. Conveniently there was also a note about Dr. Weber's *son*, who'd gone missing from his hometown around November last year. A kid by the name of Drew."

"Look," I said, but Michael waved me silent.

"She always seemed more prepared for us than she should have been," he said. "It's helpful knowing why.

And ultimately I'd say it's worked out into a result we can all be happy with. But I'm counting on you remembering my generosity over this, Drew. I still need people I can *trust*."

"It's the only thing I've ever done that went against your orders," I said. What would he understand? I thought of the glimpses I'd gotten of him with his daughter, the traces of gentleness he tried to conceal from the rest of us. "She's family. She's the only family I still have. I couldn't stand by and let her get hurt." By Nathan. By Michael, who eventually would have ramped up the pressure.

"I'm not angry," Michael said. "I'm letting you know where you stand. The ground's a little shaky, but you can deal with that. You've proven you can navigate conflicting loyalties without much fallout. That sort of ingenuity has its benefits to an organization like this. Of course, so does Nathan's penchant for violence. What I'm most interested to see is how that contrast plays out. Whether your smarts can win over his brutality when you have an entire operation to manage. Unless, as I asked before, you don't think you're up to this particular assignment?"

What could I say? It was true: Kaelyn could have decided to stay in Toronto. And if Nathan had a grudge toward me, he had one ten times bigger for her.

Besides, I had the feeling that if I said no, brutality

would win right now in the instant it'd take Michael to reach for his revolver.

"I can handle Nathan," I said. I'd better figure out how to, anyway.

"Glad to hear it," Michael said, shifting back in his chair.

I paused, and risked asking, "The relocation to Toronto... That'd be permanent?"

"You're thinking about Zachary."

I dipped my head. Not much point in denying it.

"Worry about that later," Michael said. "I'm not disinclined to reward a job well done."

That was probably as good as I could have hoped for. "Thank you," I said.

"Just make sure it does go well," he said. "I'm giving you full authority to use your judgment and implement whatever solution seems necessary if the situation goes sour. Are we understood?"

"Yes," I said. "Of course. I appreciate your confidence in me."

I had one night to say good-bye to Zack. He came by my room in the dormitory building when he finished his shift in the cafeteria. I was packing, folding my few spare T-shirts, an extra pair of jeans, and the sweater I'd held on to since leaving the island as tightly as I could so they'd fit into the moderately-sized rucksack the woman in the supply department had handed over. I needed to leave room for food and bottled water, since I didn't trust Nathan to allow me a fair share of our communal provisions, some basic survival gear like matches and a compass, in case he decided to kick me out of the car somewhere between here and Toronto, and the pistol the supply department woman had set out alongside the sack, saying Michael had requested it for me.

I didn't like the cool weight of it in my hands, didn't like even looking at it. Michael had insisted everyone here do a few lessons in the firing range, so I knew how to use it, but it was like an exclamation point on his last few words to me. *Implement whatever solution seems necessary.* He couldn't be much clearer what sort of solution he imagined might be required.

Of course, if all Michael wanted was Nathan dead and his own hands clean, he could have sent someone along he knew had killed before, who'd have no qualms about doing it again. Instead, he'd picked me.

My smarts. Nathan's brutality. *What I'm most interested to see is how that contrast plays out.* As if this was some bizarre sort of test. Testing me, testing Nathan. Testing what we stood for? Throw us into the fire and see which of us better withstood the heat.

He wanted me to win. From the way he'd phrased his remarks, I was pretty sure of that. Michael had never shied away from brutality to enforce his demands before, but with the sort of people this organization attracted and the sort of people they'd clashed with, the urgency of pulling everything together in the midst of the pandemic, he might not have seen another option.

He'd been a cop, in his former life. The things he'd done to get this far might not sit well with his conscience. Why else leave the brutality to guys like Nathan and Chay when he could? Maybe he'd like to rely more on ingenuity and less on violence to get things done. Maybe this, me and Nate in Toronto, was his trial run: removed enough from him that he could displace most of the responsibility if we—if *I*—blundered it.

I had no idea if I had enough ingenuity to maneuver Nathan as well as I'd contrived Kaelyn's safety. Given the gun, Michael didn't either. The brutal option, if I needed it.

There wasn't any getting out of his test now. I tossed the pistol on the bed, figuring it should go in the rucksack last so it'd be within easy reach if I needed it before we'd even made it to Toronto. It was still lying there when Zack knocked and I called him in. He ambled over and slid his arms around my waist from behind. I felt him noticing the gun, tensing.

I laid one of my arms over his, clay brown against freckled white. "Just in case," I said.

"Hmmm," he replied, with a kiss to the base of my neck. He'd been there when Nathan went off on me for talking to the prisoners, before I'd come up with my plan for Kaelyn's escape; had seen the purpling scrape along my ribs where Nate had introduced them to the edge of a table, after. "I guess that's what we signed up for, being here."

Zack hadn't really signed up for anything. I'd volunteered myself, with some idea what I was getting into, when I'd made it to Toronto looking for answers and seen the extent to which Michael had taken control. But Zack's mom had been given the impossible choice of either supporting Michael's efforts or wasting away in a locked room somewhere, and Zack had stayed with her—for her protection, I suspected he thought, though her expertise protected him more than the other way around. She worked long hours in the labs, helping manufacture the vaccine, but she'd arranged that Zack would never be assigned to leave the training center's walls, where the infected and the hostile survivors who hadn't joined the Wardens wandered.

She'd offered to come here when Michael had asked some of the doctors to travel south and I'd already requested a transfer so I could follow Kaelyn. Because she knew Zack and I would want to stay together. And now, a couple months later, I was turning around and heading back.

Maybe they'd follow me again. *I'm not disinclined to reward a job well done.* But that possibility hardly felt tangible right now.

"I'm sorry," I said, squeezing his hand.

Zack made a scoffing sound. "For what? Not arguing with Michael over this? I'd rather take you alive and in Canada. We'll make sure it's not forever. I'll survive somehow until then."

I nudged him with my elbow at his teasing tone. "Just keep on keeping your head down, all right?"

"I should be the one saying that to you," he said. "Look at you moving up in the ranks. One step from king of Toronto! You know what they say about power."

"Absolute power corrupts absolutely?"

He smiled against my shoulder. "I was thinking, 'With great power there must also come great responsibility.' But the other's true too."

His voice was still teasing, but I could hear the apprehension underneath. "It'll be okay," I said, for both of us. "I'll be okay."

"Do," he said simply. "Please."

I shoved the last few items in my sack and tugged the drawstring tight. Zack loosened his hold as I turned to face him. My roommate was on gate duty for another two hours. Two hours. The last time we'd really have together in who knew how long. Even tomorrow... We hadn't been hiding our relationship, but with the company we kept, it seemed safer to avoid public displays of affection.

A lump rose in my throat. "Let's not talk anymore," I said, close enough that our noses almost touched.

"What do you recommend we do instead?" he asked, a glint in his hazel eyes, and I pulled him into a kiss.

Something it was hard to miss if you spent a lot of time with people and electronics was that the two were a lot alike. People were more complicated, sure—I'd freely admit that while I could piece together a motherboard, brain surgery was beyond me—but nevertheless made up of a fairly predictable set of systems interacting with each other following fairly predictable patterns. You pushed certain buttons, you received certain reactions. Getting along with people, or getting what you needed from them, was mostly a matter of tracing the wires until you found the right connections.

At least, with most. A few people, like Michael, were so good at keeping what was going on in their heads hidden that it was hard to identify the connections at all. And others, like Nathan, seemed to rearrange their wiring on an hourly basis.

Sometimes Nate was so easy I was ashamed of how nervous he made me. Like, when I'd come down to meet him in the parking lot where Michael was overseeing the loading of the industrial coolers with our first batch of the vaccines for up north into the trailer hitched to the Mercedes' rear, I'd patted the convertible's gleaming red hood and said, "Couldn't ask for a sweeter ride," and Nathan had grinned and preened his dark brown hair and said, "Then get yourself in here," as if there'd never been any hostility between us.

We made good time cruising along the vacant highways—the snow was long gone even in the northern states now. Nathan and I didn't talk much, Nate preferring to blare club music from the convertible's speakers, but he handed off the keys to let me take over driving for a few hours with only a narrow look and a warning to forget any stunts. We stopped to meet up with a group of Wardens in Pittsburgh, who refilled the tank and the jugs we were carrying and eagerly accepted one of the vaccine coolers, and continued on across the border in the fading daylight.

As night settled in and the headlights caught on a sign announcing just a hundred more kilometers to Toronto, I was starting to think maybe Michael was even more of a genius than I'd given him credit for. Maybe sending Nathan off to run his own fiefdom was exactly what the guy needed to simmer down. If he relaxed all on his own, I could just hang back and offer my approval, no maneuvering necessary.

Then the last song on the CD faded out, and Nathan didn't immediately reach for a new one from the binder I suspected he'd found with the car. The last time we'd filled the tank, he'd pulled the top up, but he'd left his window down. The air washing in from outside had taken on an uncomfortable chill. I'd zipped up my jacket and tucked my hands into my pockets rather than complain. Nathan's narrow face and hands were pale, but then, they were always pale. It was hard to tell whether he didn't feel the cold or was making a show of how tough he was.

"You started out up here," he said.

I nodded. "I was here a couple months, mostly doing the same work as in Georgia: the radios and that."

"I want you making sure the existing establishment accepts their new management," he said. "You know them, you encourage them to see it's in their best interests not to mess with me. Do you think anyone will need extra persuading?"

If I was going to nudge Nathan toward a more diplomatic approach, I couldn't get a better opening. "I haven't seen them in a while," I said. "But the people I worked with before, they're like the Wardens down south. They don't really *like* taking orders, but they do because they can see it works to their benefit. You show you're there to lead them, not knock them down, and I don't think there'll be any trouble."

"You sound like a shrink," Nathan said. "I don't care what they *like*. They'd better be prepared to get knocked down if they don't get in line fast."

"Michael's informed them we're coming. They'll be ready for the change."

Nathan's mouth curled into a sneer. "What kind of ready, we'll see." He shot me a look, his eyes shadowed in the dim light that reached us from the headlights. "We need to watch out for ourselves up here. This is going to be *my* city, and that's just the beginning. You prove yourself, I'll keep you along."

"Hey," I said, backing off any intention other than gratifying him, "you've the one who's here, not Michael. I know who I'm taking *my* orders from."

His sneer jerked into a scowl. "Whatever Michael tells you to do, you do," he snapped. "I don't want to be picking up your slack."

"Right," I said. "Of course not. That won't be a problem."

He turned the music back on, and I resolved to keep my mouth shut for the rest of the drive. Maybe once we got settled in, and I'd been around him longer, I'd get better at predicting what he wanted to hear.

Or maybe, with Nathan, sometimes there was never going to be a right answer.

*   *   *

Since I'd left the city, the local Wardens had moved headquarters to one of the larger fire stations, with the rescue vehicles cleared out to make room for their assortment of cars and trucks and a large storage area. The inner circle of Wardens lived in the station's dorms, and close associates in the low-rise apartment building next door. Janelle, the sharp-eyed woman with a boxer's build who'd been at the top of the hierarchy when I left, had obviously gotten the message about the new leadership. Two of the dorm rooms had been vacated to give both Nathan and me a private space, while everyone else was doubling up. But after the long hours in the car with Nate's uncertain temper, I didn't have the energy to wonder who we'd displaced or do anything other than offer a few greetings before I crashed onto the cot at half past midnight.

The Wardens had reorganized elsewhere as well, in anticipation of our cargo. When I strolled into the common room the next morning, I noted the industrial refrigeration unit set against the wall, which the vaccine vials would have already been unloaded into. Janelle was sitting at one of the tables, eyeing the fridge over the top of her coffee mug. She turned her piercing gaze on me.

"Some of those doses had better be for us," she said.

True to his word, Michael had given his very first

batches of the vaccine to those on the compound in Georgia. I expected his orders here were similar, but he'd given them to Nathan, not to me. It was a little early to risk stepping on the boss's toes.

Of course, Janelle's bad side wasn't a great place to be either. I'd seen her break a guy's nose for mouthing off.

"I think so," I said. "You've got a doctor prepped to do the administering?"

"A couple. They'll set up shop in here, once we let them know they're needed."

"I'd imagine we'll get started right away."

"A lot of people out there already waiting for it," she said with a raise of her chin toward the front doors. An edge crept into her voice. "You two are the head honchos now. You just say the word."

"I don't think it was a criticism of your work," I offered. "Michael just wanted people in place who are a little more familiar with the vaccine. Anyway, it looks like you've got everything in good order already."

Finally she gave me a hint of a smile. "Hard to believe it's actually happening," she said. "No more friendly flu! I'm looking forward to having that worry off my back."

"The doctors are saying we should keep up the basic precautions, face masks and that, in case it doesn't give total immunity," I said. "But yeah. It's a good feeling."

A couple Wardens were posted in the entry hall. I peered past them through the glass doors, and saw what Janelle had meant about the people waiting. Word had obviously gotten around that the vaccine was on its way. A couple teens in ratty clothes were sitting on the edge of the sidewalk outside, eyeing the building, and a middle-aged woman was pacing back and forth across the road, darting glances this way.

Nathan stalked into the common room just after I stepped back, his cheeks and jaw pink from a fresh shave. He was wearing one of his usual slim suits, this one silvery gray. "All right," he said, rubbing his hands together. "I want the troops in here a-sap so I can lay down the ground rules."

Janelle headed to the radio room. "I'll call everyone in," she said.

"Nathan," I said while she could overhear, "some of the vaccine is set aside for the Wardens here, isn't it?"

"You're getting ahead of me," he said in a tone that walked the line between amused and irritated. "Anyone who deserves it will get it. We should see what sort of response we get to the initial announcement before we go dividing up what we have. Milk everything we can from the saps out there who want their hands on it right away."

Janelle's mouth tightened. Nathan was forgetting how desperate the people in *here* might be. Neither of us was going to make any progress toward Michael's goals if we turned our supporters against us on the very first day.

"Good point," I said carefully. "Could help us police things, though, if none of us has to worry about getting infected. It seemed like it gave us an extra edge in Georgia. But that's more your area."

His lips curled into a smirk. Remembering some recent exploit of his own, tangling with outside survivors, I'd bet. I wandered off toward the kitchen as if it didn't matter much to me either way. As I reached the doorway, Nate turned to Janelle.

"We'll start with our people. But I want to hear if there's anyone you think should be left hanging a little while to consider their options."

"Sure thing," she said, and ducked out. I exhaled and kept walking.

Within an hour we had a crowd of thirty or so in the common room. The two doctors Janelle had mentioned were among them, laying out the equipment they had on hand—syringes and liquid antiseptic and the like—on a table near the entry hall. The crowd was mostly focused on that, muttering to each other and stirring restlessly.

"Listen up," Nathan said at the head of the room, spreading his arms wide like a stage magician. "We've got the most valuable merchandise currently in existence, and we need to price it accordingly. When you're making the rounds, I want you passing on word that the vaccine is available to anyone able to buy it—but supplies are limited, so they'd better get here fast and with a generous spirit." He grinned. "Michael said· he sent on a list of acceptable payments?"

Janelle nodded and held up a paper with scrawled notations.

"Good," Nathan said. "*On top* of that, as our starting point, I expect anyone who wants that vaccine to give over either two gallons of gasoline or diesel, or a working gun, or a box of ammunition. Gas or gun, or they don't get the shot."

Janelle frowned, and a guy named Tyler, who'd been working in the radio room, stepped forward.

"Michael didn't say anything about that," he said. "We've already been spreading the word—people are crazy for the vaccine—it could get uglier than it needs to if we tell them they've got to give even more."

"I'm glad you brought that up," Nathan said, still smiling. Then with a flick of his wrist, his switchblade was open in his hand, arcing out to slash across Tyler's face. Tyler flinched, too slow to avoid it. He stumbled back, clutching his chin, a few drops of blood seeping from beneath his fingers to patter onto the floor.

"You can listen to Michael, who's hundreds of miles away, or you can listen to the guy who's right in front of you, who can do that or worse if he wants," Nathan said. He held the knife casually, waggling the handle. "*I* decide what needs to happen. And I think I'm deciding that your vaccination can be put off a few days." He glanced around the room. "Any more complaints?"

Tyler's face clenched, as if he was considering taking a lunge at Nathan, but his gaze seemed to catch on the light glinting off the blade. Janelle had straightened up, her frown deepened, but she didn't speak either. Everyone just eyed Nathan warily. Violence was a power everyone here understood.

What he'd just said, it sounded too much like what I'd said to him in the car—the comment he'd bitten my head off over. Had I given him that idea? That wasn't the direction I'd meant to push him in.

No, the way he'd been talking even before then, he'd planned to assert his authority from the start. I had a lot of work ahead of me.

Janelle cleared her throat. "There's something else we need to talk about," she said. "A group of locals has set up their own little outfit, gathering supplies, policing the neighborhood they're settled in. We had an issue with them early on, but after we showed how easily we could massacre them, the ones we didn't cut down have been kowtowing. Michael told us to let them keep on like that as long as they didn't make another move on us—we've been able to use them a few times when we've needed something big done. They've been angling for priority on the vaccine."

Nathan guffawed. "And give our competition a step up? We'd be better off if the virus got them. They can get in line with everyone else—and I want *them* paying double."

Janelle's eyebrows rose. Nathan flicked his switchblade in and out of its handle. "Is there a problem with that?" he inquired when she didn't immediately speak. "Your people here *can* keep this outfit under control, can't they? I expected a solid operation here."

"We can handle them just fine," Janelle said, but when he turned away, she glowered at him.

So we had another group of thugs who'd be looking to take out their frustrations on us. That was just great. And if the truce fell apart, Michael wasn't going to restrict blame to Nathan.

I could at least make sure we were solid here. "I guess we should get everyone started on their shots so they can get to work," I said to Nathan, trying to sound as if I was supporting him, not directing.

"Sure, sure," Nathan said. "Get yourselves inoculated and then get on it. You have your marching orders." He pointed to Tyler. "Except you. Let's see how I feel about your 'performance' by tomorrow."

He spun on his heel and strode out of the room.

*   *   *

Our payments started arriving later that morning: dry and canned food, basic medications, electronics we could still make use of, and of course the gas and the guns. Nathan prowled the common room as people trickled in through the entry hall. He wanted the extra fuel and weaponry set aside so he could stow them elsewhere.

"Where do you think you're going with that?" he barked at a Warden who looked younger than Kaelyn, who'd been carting a couple jugs of diesel through the common room.

"Putting the stuff away," the girl said, looking puzzled.

Nathan reached out and grasped a hunk of her hair, twisting it with a yank until she cried out. "Next time you screw up it's coming right out," he said, drawing his arm back and wiping his hand on his jacket. He pointed to the room that held his personal stash. "That 'stuff' goes over *there*."

No one else said anything as the girl hustled off, but the tension in the air made the hair on the back of my neck rise.

He sent me off on the second day with a personal assignment: "You lived here," he said. "Find me a secure storage space."

I thought it'd be a relief to leave the fire station for a while. But leaving, I had to pass the stragglers lingering outside, empty-handed or with bundles of goods deemed not quite enough payment to be accepted. An old man was sitting in the courtyard sobbing. A mother was trying to corral her two scrawny little kids while begging everyone who approached to spare something for her so she could pay for their shots. "Please," she said, extending her hand to me, and I automatically shook my head and muttered, "Sorry." The moment squeezed around my gut like a clenched fist as I walked on.

I'd spent most of my teens exploring these streets in the five years Dad's job had transplanted us here. Weaving through them now stirred up memories of a person I'd let myself forget. I'd rallied in this square with hundreds of other protesters, shouting and brandishing my poster board. I'd stood by this statue wheedling passersby into signing a petition. Mom used to say that I'd always been a crusader—even when the only injustice I was trying to defeat was the fact that Kaelyn had gotten a slightly bigger piece of my fifth birthday cake, a story she'd never gotten tired of telling —but it was in this city that I'd really woken up to the world beyond the island. To what sort of people I wanted to kiss and date, and how many other people had a problem with that. To the privilege allotted to me because I could be mistaken for a white guy with a dark tan, and how many walls could go up when I wasn't.

I had ranted and raged, and looking back I had the feeling I'd been an exceptionally difficult kid to live with. But it had been important. I'd wanted to set things *right*.

Now I was nineteen, not a kid anymore, and I wasn't sure where that kid had gone. Zack had encouraged me to keep my head down, with no idea I used to be the kind of guy who'd call out people who just looked the other way.

It wasn't that *world* anymore. I was still trying to set things right, I just... couldn't approach it the same way. Taking a stand on my own would have gotten me killed. I'd needed a platform to work from, and I'd gotten myself one by insinuating myself with Michael—as far as that had taken me. I'd saved Kaelyn's life more than once, helped her get the vaccine to the CDC.

But even Michael didn't like the way we were running things, apparently, and looking around me, I could understand it. Most of the people we were ruling over didn't need brutality to keep them in line. They were already crushed. The Wardens *could* ease back— we could be guardians here instead of tyrants, earning respect instead of spreading fear, without losing one bit of the hold we'd gained. We could be helping rebuild this city instead of terrorizing it.

I could imagine that, but I couldn't imagine how to maneuver Nathan into going for it. I did know the person I'd used to be wouldn't have been content to slowly nudge the situation in that direction from behind the scenes. That kid would have been furious at the way Nathan was exploiting the survivors who needed the vaccine, at the suffering the Wardens were prolonging right outside the walls of the building that kept *me* secure, not pretending to be okay with it.

Maybe I was furious, under that twist of guilt. Maybe I'd just gotten too good at stifling any emotions I'd have to hide. The fire I'd used to have was in there somewhere.

I wanted it back.

I returned to the station with Nathan's assignment accomplished and my own wires in better order. Enough tiptoeing around. It was time to push Nate harder.

"I think you'll approve," I said to him when we arrived at the place I'd picked out: what had once been a clothing shop just a few blocks from the station. The building was an older construction, boards and nails instead of bars and concrete, but sturdy. The idea that his stash wouldn't be totally inaccessible had given me a particle of reassurance.

I pointed to the front windows. "Those shutters are steel, so no one's going to break in that way. And both the front door and the delivery entrance at the back are reinforced. You can drop things off around back without anyone on the street noticing, so chances are good no one's even going to realize there's any point in trying to break in." I motioned to the FOR RENT sign. "The business must have gone under before the flu— their inventory's cleared out, so there's plenty of room."

"It's close to the freeway too," Nathan murmured to himself as we headed down the back alley to the delivery entrance. Was he planning on taking off somewhere with his stash? He'd suggested that control of this city was just the start—it could be he was thinking he could swallow up more and more of Michael's territory until he had the means to take on what remained of Michael's operation directly.

How did I steer him away from that? What was his point of leverage? To really move a person, you had to know where they were coming from.

"So what did you do, before all this?" I asked, aiming for a conversational tone, as Nathan hauled open the garage-like door. I considered his suit: today, sleek navy. "Some kind of business exec thing?"

Nathan chuckled. "Something like that."

"You must miss it."

He scanned the inner space of the inventory area, and then shot me a narrow look. "Is this supposed to be a heart-to-heart? Save that for your boyfriend." He stepped out, glanced up and down the alley, and grinned. "I don't miss anything."

Because it was easier to grab power now that it all relied on who had the biggest knife and the fastest draw?

Nathan yanked down the door and prodded the edges. I was considering what angle to take that wouldn't end in a conversation with his switchblade when he nodded, said, "It'll do," and stalked back to his convertible without so much as a backward glance. No praise, no thank you. No further opening. He was pulling away from the curb as I followed him out of the alley.

Well, that hadn't gotten me very far. At least it was only five minutes to the station. I preferred the walk to his company.

I'd made it two blocks, stewing over possible overtures, when a different car pulled up alongside me: a dark blue BMW sedan. I paused, keeping a careful distance from both the car and the buildings beside me, in case this was some kind of ambush. I'd been carrying the pistol in my jacket—*Just in case*, like I'd said to Zack —and a pocket knife in my jeans. In a hand-to-hand struggle I'd probably have better luck with the knife. I dropped my hand to rest over the pocket.

The car's front passenger window rolled down and a tall, ropey-muscled guy with a mane of tangled black hair leaned his arm out. I relaxed slightly. I'd seen him in the station, arguing with Janelle—Trang, she'd called him. He was someone higher up in that local gang she'd told us about. The Strikers, they went by, for whatever reason.

"I hear you can speak for Michael," Trang said in a reedy voice that sounded odd coming from such a hulking figure. The guy in the driver's seat peered past him at me.

"To some extent," I said.

He motioned to the driver, who cut the gas. Trang stepped out and propped himself against the side of the car with the door still open. Leaving the driver a clear shot at me if he needed it? Nice.

"We've gone along with the way you people want to run things," Trang said. "We've helped out when asked. Now the new boss in town is insulting *our* people to their faces, demanding we hand over more than anyone else in the city to get that vaccine? Maybe you can tell me what message Michael is trying to pass on. Because if it's the one we're getting, I know what we're going to say back. And we'll be using more than our words."

"I heard that approach didn't go so well for you last time," I said, keeping my voice even.

"Maybe we backed down too soon," Trang said. "Maybe we're thinking we'd rather take some of you with us than bow down just to be ground under some jerk-off's heel."

At a glance, his stance against the car would have

looked casual, but tension was coiled through his posture, the angle of his shoulders, the flexing of his arms. I believed the threat. But they'd bowed down this long. They had some kind of a survival instinct.

"Look," I said. "The attitude, the pricing—that's all Nathan. He and Michael have some... differences of opinion that we're in the process of sorting out. If you give it a little more time for words to work, we'll all come out better off, don't you think?"

Trang studied me for a long moment. "You don't talk like the rest of them," he said.

"I'm not like the rest of them," I replied. "That's why Michael sent me."

After another few seconds, he inclined his head and swung back into the car. "All right," he said. "But don't make us wait too long."

I had to work faster. But Nathan wasn't making it easy. I went to the store with him twice over the next few days to unload the small delivery van he was having the Wardens pack his gas and guns into now, but he made me drive the van while he took the convertible—"Waste of *our* gas," I overheard Janelle muttering, but Nate seemed to think it made a necessary statement—and while I was hefting the boxes he scrawled numbers on them and on the wall of the storage area with chalk, murmuring to himself. He snapped at me when I attempted conversation. It looked like he was tallying up his haul, but there were other, larger numbers on the wall next to them. His goals?

"That's my job; focus on yours," he said when I asked.

Other than that, I barely saw him. He'd started taking his meals at odd times when no one else was likely to be in the kitchen, and the one time I happened to walk in while he taking a bowl out of the microwave, he immediately sauntered out with it. He left in his convertible for an hour or two at a time a few times a day, without saying where he was going. But we were never really free of him either. He lurked, popping into the common room unexpectedly to watch the Wardens on duty truck off vaccine payments and to announce changes to the patrol schedule at a moment's notice.

We'd been in the city six days when I was heading up to the dormitory and heard hushed voices at the top of the stairwell. I paused just before the bend.

"I didn't *do* anything," a young man's voice was saying, choked up with anger. "He comes barging in, saying I let that tank leak all over—it's not *my* fault the idiot who paid with it didn't screw the cap on properly."

"So check them more carefully from now on," Janelle's voice responded. Then it softened slightly. "He shouldn't have done that."

"I should take his whole *ear* off," the guy she was

talking to said. "Both of them."

"Devon, you know you have to—"

She halted when I came around the bend and continued up. Devon was holding a rag to the side of his head. A bloody rag.

"What's going on?" I asked.

"Nothing," Devon said, and skulked off. I glanced at Janelle.

"Nathan cut his earlobe off," she said flatly, and then she walked away too.

They didn't trust me enough to criticize him in front of me. Why should they? Michael had sent us together. Of course they'd assume I was Nate's lackey. I hadn't done much to prove otherwise.

The next morning I came down to grab breakfast and found Tyler appealing to Nathan outside the radio room.

"Our supply's almost gone," he was saying, keeping his voice quiet and his head low. "I wanted to ask if you'd reconsidered—"

"Look at you," Nathan interrupted with a sneer. "I don't know why I'd want someone like you in my outfit anyway. Maybe if you can survive long enough for the second shipment to get in."

Tyler paled even as his eyes narrowed. "Just tell me what you want me to do," he said.

"I want you to wait," Nathan said, and noticed me

watching. "Yes, Drew?"

I didn't see any point in continuing to withhold Tyler's shot, other than whatever malicious pleasure Nathan got out of the power trip. The guy hadn't made a peep of protest since that first day, to Nate or me, and from what I'd seen he handled himself efficiently in the radio room. But Nathan had edged his question like a knife. In the space of my hesitation, I couldn't find a way to express my disagreement that I didn't think would just set Nate even more firmly in his tracks—and set back any progress I'd made in earning *his* trust.

"Just passing through," I said, and ducked into the kitchen biting my tongue.

I didn't look at Tyler when he stalked in a minute later and banged a mug down on the counter, but I was aware of him on my periphery as I gulped down the oatmeal the guy on morning meal duty had cooked up. I still couldn't think of how I could have handled Nathan better just now. So much for my "smarts." How could I get a foothold with him when he was keeping himself too removed to even touch?

How would I have tackled a figure like him in my former life?

I turned that idea over as I finished my bowl. Someone at the top of the food chain, a CEO or politician, I'd never have aimed at straight on. I'd have known there was no point and focused on rallying other people until there were enough of us to force a change.

The Wardens were already unhappy. If I had their loyalty, if they'd stand behind me in standing up to Nate... Michael had never said I couldn't simply displace him.

I washed the bowl, chucked it on the rack, and turned to face Tyler. "Come with me," I said.

He eyed me over the top of his mug. When I tilted my head toward the door, he got up. I led the way to the vaccination table, where the doctors were passing a creased entertainment magazine back and forth while waiting for our next customer.

"It's his turn," I said, in a tone I hoped conveyed sufficient authority, as I jerked my thumb toward Tyler.

They looked from me to him and back again. Tyler just stared at me.

"From what I heard, the guy in charge—" one started, and I cut him off.

"Sometimes the guy in charge needs a little help taking the right course. That's what second in commands are for. Give him the shot."

My heart was thumping so hard I crossed my arms over my chest not just for emphasis but also to make sure my hands didn't tremble. If Nate walked in now, I'd lose more than an earlobe. But he didn't. The doctor got out a syringe and gave Tyler his vaccination, and Tyler let out a sharp laugh of relief.

"If anyone asks, you're still waiting," I told him while the doctors could hear. My safety was assured in the fact that any of them would be in just as much trouble as me if Nathan found out. Tyler nodded, looking at me with a keenness that hadn't been there before.

I smiled, the fading surge of adrenaline leaving me energized. I could build on this. A spark of an idea lit in my head.

"Grab a few of the people around and meet me back here as quickly as you can," I said. "I've got a job for us to take care of."

Twenty minutes later, Tyler, three of the other Wardens, and one of the doctors stopped with me outside the three-story row house I'd noticed the woman with the two kids disappearing into a few days ago. I'd kept an eye on it during my wanderings as I'd re-familiarized myself with the neighborhood in its flu-altered state. At least one other family with young kids was holed up in there—I'd seen a white-haired man who might have been a grandfather ushering a little girl inside while cradling a baby in his arms.

This "job" didn't technically require anyone except me, the doctor, and the case of filled syringes I'd told her to bring along, but I wanted an audience, and I wanted to observe how that audience responded.

I knocked on the door, the others shuffling their feet

on the sidewalk behind me. It was the older man who
answered, opening it just a crack.

"We're making a house call," I said. "Limited time
special offer. Any kids here under thirteen can get a
shot payment-free. Can we come in?"

Someone behind me snorted, maybe thinking we
didn't need to bother asking. Not an attitude I planned
to encourage. The man's gaze slid from me to the doctor
to the case in her hands. He backed up, opening the
door wider.

We ended up in the cluttered first floor living room
—no one had been keeping the place neat, and
crumpled food packaging bags and cartons lay strewn
around the sagging couch and heaped along the walls.
The old man, who still hadn't said anything to us,
brought the little girl and her baby brother in. The
woman I'd seen begging outside the station peeked in
with her two boys, and a girl who looked to be about
ten crept in just as we were finishing with those four.
Thankfully, that was it, because I'd only had the doctor
bring five doses.

Tyler and the others slouched by the doorway as the
doctor did her work. I'd have gotten more satisfaction
out of seeing the anxiety on the kids' faces giving way to
hope if I hadn't sensed skepticism in my colleagues
every time I glanced their way.

"What about us?" the woman said after we were

done.

"*What about us?*" one of the Wardens mocked in a singsong voice, and she cringed.

I shot him a pointed look, and he just grinned. "*You* should be able to scavenge up something," I said. "This was just for the kids who can't fend for themselves—be glad we offered that."

I wanted to add that I was going to try to cut down the payments, that none of this had been my idea in the first place, but that might encourage them to start arguing down at the station where they could draw Nathan's attention—and irritation.

"You give a little, they want everything," one of my colleagues said as we headed back. "What a bunch of freeloaders."

"It'd get Nathan's goat if he knew, though," the guy who'd done the mocking earlier said, and high-fived Tyler. Then he turned to me. "What else do you have in mind?"

So that's what they assumed this was about— sticking it to Nathan?

"There's no reason anyone in this city needs to die from the friendly flu now that the vaccine's being made," I said. "And it doesn't cost us anything to give it to people who couldn't pay us anyway."

The woman arched an eyebrow, and Tyler laughed, as if he thought I was making a joke. "I guess it's good to make sure we have a good pool of grunts to do the heavy lifting down the line," the other guy remarked. "They'll be able to pay their way later on, right?"

"Yeah," I said, playing to that attitude with a growing queasiness. "Worse for us if the kids get sick, too—parents can go kind of crazy trying to save them."

What kind of future did they envision here? A world where the Wardens lorded our power over everyone else for as long as we could, until there wasn't anything left to scavenge or stockpile and our own stores ran out—and then what?

I wasn't sure they were bothering to think that far. Looking at them right now, I wasn't sure they *cared* what happened to anyone else as long as they were living in comfort. Maybe I'd been naive to think it might be otherwise. Even in their former lives, most of the Wardens had been surviving by screwing over whomever they could. Anyone who did have some compassion, some desire to see us form something that resembled an actual society again... they'd have learned to bury those impulses just like I had.

Whatever approval I'd earned just now, it was because I'd gone against a guy they hated, not because I'd demonstrated a better way of ruling. That might be enough to inspire them to turn on Nathan, but it wasn't going to convince them to bow to me in his place. What could I do that they'd respect, that *didn't* involve treating Nathan just as brutally as he was treating the rest of them?

This was Michael's real problem. It wasn't our "subjects" he was hesitant to back off on. It was his own supporters. If after everything he'd accomplished, he wasn't sure he could ease off, show a little kindness, without the Wardens jumping on that as a weakness, what hope in hell did I have?

"If I need you again, I'll know I can call on you," I told the others as the station came into view. I watched them saunter on ahead, feeling just as uncertain as before.

The knock on my dorm room door came early the next morning, just after I'd gotten up.

"Yeah?" I said, tugging my shirt the rest of the way over my head.

Nathan peered inside. My skin prickled at the idea of him coming into this tight space, but I gave him the respectful nod I knew he expected. He looked calm enough. Probably he just wanted me to haul another load of gas and guns for him. He left the door ajar as he stepped inside, which reassured me further. I should have known better.

"You've made yourself at home," he said breezily, glancing at my sparse assortment of clothes hung on the wall hooks, the crate I was using as a bedside table with a couple books I'd unofficially borrowed from the neighborhood library.

"Seems like we're going to be here a while," I said.

"Hmmm," he said, cocking his head. Then he lunged.

His forearm socked me across the chest, elbow to the ribs, slamming me into the wall. I choked on my breath as the cool edge of his switchblade touched my throat. I pressed my head back, away from it, instinctively.

Nathan leaned in, his eyes flat. My heart pounded. I had a few inches on him, and he was nearly as thin as I was—I probably could have thrown him off if it'd been a fair fight. If I hadn't felt the bite of metal nicking my skin when I swallowed.

"I hear you've been telling the troops it's really you calling the shots," he said, so close a fleck of spit hit my cheek.

"That's ridiculous," I said, fighting to keep my voice steady. Technically I wasn't even lying. I hadn't said that in so many words. And if he was focused on that, that probably meant no one had spilled the details of what I'd orchestrated behind his back.

"Why would I be telling them lies?" I hurried on. "Even if I wanted to, I'd know it'd get back to you. And I don't want to be calling the shots."

"You keep your eyes open and your mouth shut,

and you do what I say," Nathan said as if he hadn't heard a single word. "That's your only job here. Michael's hardly kept these cretins in line as it is."

"I haven't said anything," I protested, my voice hitching as the blade dug a little deeper. A droplet slid down my throat to my collarbone. "You're in charge. They're all yours. I don't *want* them." In that moment, *that* had never been more true.

For a second I thought he was going to do it. His mouth twisted and his shoulders braced. I could already feel, with a chill washing through me, the way the knife would slice clean into my neck, the gush of blood, the shock of pain. Then he shifted back, just an inch.

"Good," he said. "I'm going to help you remember how much you don't want it."

He pressed the blade in an arc from one corner of my jaw down across my throat to the other corner, splitting my skin in a thin, stinging line. A dribble of blood, not a gush. My hands leapt to cover it as he stepped aside.

"Remember," he said again, and stalked out.

I grabbed my least favorite T-shirt to stop the bleeding, sat down on the cot, and stared at the wall. The stinging deepened into an ache that radiated through my body. My hand holding the shirt was quivering.

If this was a test, I was almost definitely failing it.

Had I controlled that situation at all? Maybe I'd managed to blurt out the right thing to diffuse Nathan's anger. Or maybe he'd only ever intended to give a warning. Maybe he'd never even believed I'd spoken against him, just seen it as a convenient excuse to mess with my head.

There were several words I'd have had for Michael right now, even with that damned revolver on his desk. *He* hadn't wanted to deal with Nathan, so he'd handed the problem off to me. Well, it was still going to be Michael's problem if I ended up with my throat slit and Nate brought the whole Toronto operation crashing down.

Then what? Michael would take it as definite proof that ingenuity and evenhandedness couldn't work?

That was too much responsibility for anyone.

The thought reminded me of Zack's comment, the night before I left. *With great power...* God, did I wish he was here, ribbing me and quoting his comic books. Reminding me with his solid presence that I wasn't the only person left with a sense of morality. That at least one person would care if I died.

I bowed my head. A few speckles of my blood dappled the floor. My door was still ajar. Anyone walking by could have seen our altercation. I stretched out my leg to kick it shut.

I didn't really wish Zack was in the middle of this,

his life on the line as much as mine was. But knowing that didn't quench the longing that had risen up. There was *no one* I could talk to here. My probing conversations yesterday had revealed that. I wanted Zack. I wanted my family. Mom, with that calm but firm tone that said her pacifism didn't make her a pushover. Dad, who despite how much we'd argued, would have sat down and helped me analyze the facts.

I'd never had a chance to ask Kaelyn how he'd died.

I knew what *she* would say. I could remember clearly the tenor of her voice amid the crackle of radio static when she'd asked how I could have joined Michael. *What the hell are you doing?* The look on her face when she'd accused me of choosing the Wardens over her, because I'd stayed back rather than run with her to the CDC.

Then, I'd been so sure the ends justified the means. I could compromise a few morals if it allowed me to stay alive and to protect her too. My skill with electronics had kept me off the streets. Kept me from having to threaten and steal and kill with my own hands, like most of the Wardens did. Which didn't make my hands exactly clean, but it was a stain I'd been able to live with. Even hearing about the girl who'd been shot during Kaelyn's escape, a girl whose name I'd never gotten, I'd told myself I was doing all I could. That I didn't really have a choice, any more than Zack had.

But that wasn't true. As Michael had said, there was always a choice. I looked at my jacket hanging on the wall, the lump of the pistol in its pocket. *What the hell was I doing?* Michael had given me the means and his permission to destroy Nathan. Every day Nate was out there antagonizing everyone he spoke to, I was allowing that to happen. Because the other choice would make me an outright murderer.

I'd thought I was so freaking smart, joining the Wardens, creating change from the inside. Forgetting that I'd never actually worked from the inside before. I had no practice at playing things this way. All my experience was from the outside, against the status quo —where everyone around me was on my side, not another enemy. It was a miracle I'd survived this long.

My attention shifted to the rucksack lying by the cot, my small stash of extra food, the matchbox, the compass. I could take off. That was a choice too. Try to recreate the dynamic I was used to, call up the other survivors who were tired of the Wardens' tyranny.

Before I'd even finished picturing it, I knew it wouldn't work. We'd had a measure of safety before with the presence of police, the media, laws that prevented the powers that be from crushing those who opposed them. That was all gone. Any good I'd done, any wrongs I'd righted with my speeches and petitions, that was all gone too. The sting of pain along my throat made those efforts seem pathetic. If I walked out of here, by tomorrow every Warden in the city would have orders to kill me on sight. Anyone standing with me they'd massacre like they had the Strikers in those early altercations. I couldn't talk my way out of that.

I pulled the shirt away from my neck. A splotchy red line colored the fabric. I put on my jacket, folding the collar up to hide the wound, and slipped out to the bathroom.

The bleeding appeared to have stopped. I washed the cut with soap and covered it again. The last thing I needed was the other Wardens seeing how Nathan had marked me—how incapable I'd been of stopping him.

The gun was a steady weight in the side of the jacket. At this point, it wouldn't be so much murder as self-defense.

When I walked into the common room, the guys carrying off the latest payments and standing guard by the vaccination table glanced at me and then glanced away again. My skin tightened. *Had* someone seen and already spread the word? I resisted the urge to adjust my collar.

Janelle was in the kitchen, rinsing a plate. "You said you have a practice range set up here?" I said when she turned.

"You're wanting to work on your shot?" she said dryly.

"Seems like a good idea, these days."

Her gaze dipped to my neck, and then I was sure everyone knew. I guessed I could kiss good-bye any fragment of respect I'd managed to gain. My teeth gritted, but she didn't comment, only tilted her head.

"I'll show you. I wouldn't mind blowing a few things away today."

The range was set up at one end of the apparatus bay, sectioned off from the garage area by partitions that must have been lifted from some office building. Janelle showed me how to load the practice ammunition they'd found, and we set up a couple rows of emptied cans and other containers along the tables that stood near the back wall.

Her weapon of choice was a heavy revolver. She planted herself, aimed, and knocked off five targets with just a beat in between. I adjusted my fingers around the pistol's grip and trigger. Sighted. Missed the first can by at least a foot. Janelle rubbed her mouth as if she were covering a smirk.

"Been a while?" she said.

Only two months since I'd done my training, but those lessons obviously hadn't stuck. I repositioned myself and tried again. Nicked the mouth of a jar enough to send it smashing to the floor. That was satisfying. I sucked in a breath and fired off three rounds, setting the can clattering, missing another, and hitting a cereal box dead center. I paused, feeling a little pleased with that one, and raised the pistol one more time. Imagined that last can was Nathan's face. I pictured him sneering at me. My arm twitched as I pulled the trigger.

"Close," Janelle said.

I watched as she reloaded and blasted away the rest of her targets, as well as a couple of mine. She lowered her arms with a thin smile. She could do it, I thought. If Nathan pushed her hard enough, she'd snap.

That wasn't the answer, though. Mutiny would be bad for discipline, bad for morale. If one of the Wardens killed Michael's representative without Michael's backing, they were setting themselves against Michael too, and that would be an even bigger mess.

It had to be me.

I wondered what Nate would think if he saw me here with the pistol in my hands. He'd probably laugh. Say, "Bring it on." He *lived* for this. What had Michael called it? A "penchant for violence." I looked down at the gun, and my stomach turned.

"You want another go?" Janelle asked.

"No," I said, shoving the pistol back in my pocket. "I'm good."

I wasn't. But killing Nathan couldn't be the only answer. If I let him push me to that, I'd still be failing. I'd be proving his way right even as I took him down.

* * *

Nathan called on me to help him transport the latest influx of his personal supplies late that afternoon without any nod to our recent confrontation. He didn't want anyone else knowing where he was stockpiling the stuff—and maybe that performance with the knife had only been a blip in *his* day. I drove the delivery van over and unpacked it while he stalked around the storage area, muttering to himself like always. Despite the numbers he'd marked on the outside of the boxes, he still opened and sifted through them before seeming satisfying. Or somewhere close to satisfied. I was sure now the figures he'd marked on the walls, whether they were goals or something else, were a lot higher than they'd been five days ago.

"You've almost filled the place already," I commented when I'd hefted the last of the gas tanks onto the tower in one corner. Since relying on the gun or the other Wardens were both out, I had to focus on Nathan again. I'd accomplished what I had before by getting Michael to trust me and then directing events that had come into my control. Maybe I hadn't tried hard enough with Nate. I wasn't giving up.

"We can use the front room next," Nathan said with a frown. "And then there's upstairs."

I glanced at the stairwell, steep steps showing raw wood where the paint had been worn down. While he said "we," I'd be doing the heavy lugging. Well, building a little muscle couldn't be a bad thing these days. Although...

"It'd be easier to move everything in a hurry if you took over one of the places next door and stuck to the lower levels," I said, remembering his remark before about the vicinity of the freeway. "If that's part of your plan for all this." I kept my tone carefully light.

"Always have plans," Nathan said, staring at the numbers on the wall. "Always be one step ahead."

I supposed that was a kind of answer. "I agree," I said. "And you know, if you find you need more or less of a specific thing, I'll make sure the collection guys adjust their payment instructions."

He turned, and I braced for him to tell me off. But apparently I hadn't pushed quite too far. All he said, evenly, was, "Thank you, but I can talk to them myself."

"Well, Michael put me at your disposal," I said, risking a little more. "Just trying to make sure I'm pulling my weight."

He smiled then, with a manic quality that made me regret the comment.

"You'll know when I need more from you," he said. "As long as you've proven you're ready."

"What would 'ready' look like?" I asked as we walked back to the vehicles. "If there *is* something else you want me to be taking care of..."

"Ready would include knowing without having to ask," Nathan snapped, and hopped into his convertible.

I pulled into the station just behind him and followed him up to the common room. A trio of Strikers had just come into the entry hall, wearing yellow cloths tied around their biceps to identify themselves. They'd been showing up in small groups as they gathered the extra resources to meet Nathan's inflated vaccine price. This trio had pushed in a couple trolleys stacked with boxes with a grocery store logo, a few 5-gallon gasoline tanks, and a carton of ammo. The Wardens at the inner door were looking it over, one inspecting the boxes' contents while the other stood poised with her submachine gun. I paused, thinking I could make a show of confirming Nathan's haul went to the right place while he was here to see it.

Nathan strolled right over. He nudged one of the gasoline tanks with the toe of his black leather Oxford and his lip curled disdainfully.

"Not enough," he said.

The Strikers stared at him. "What do you mean?" said the guy closest to Nathan, his thin eyebrows pulling together. "This is everything we were asked for."

"The price just went up," Nathan announced. "Come back with twice that, and you can have your shots."

The three barely moved, but I caught the way their

bodies shifted: shoulders squaring, hands dipping a little closer to concealed weapons. What was Nathan thinking? He'd already doubled their price once.

"Says who?" one of the Strikers asked, almost a snarl.

"Says the guy who runs this city," Nathan said. *He* didn't look ready for a fight. But then, Nathan pretty much always was, without any indication at all. Even so, there were three of them. I got a flash of an image: the Strikers bursting into the common room, a hail of bullets from both sides, blood all across the floor...

I pulled my spine up as straight as it would go and strode over. "Is there a problem?" I said, fixing my gaze on the Striker who'd last spoken.

The trio glanced from Nathan to me. "*I* don't think there's a problem," Nathan said with a warning edge. He didn't like me interfering—I could be undoing any small gains I'd established with him earlier. But his good will wasn't going to solve *my* problems if a gang war broke out today.

"I say we shouldn't have to pay anything," the first Striker muttered, and the guard lifted her gun.

"I don't see what you need the vaccine for if you're determined to die in the next thirty seconds," I remarked, and then, to Nathan, "Sorry. Obviously you can handle these idiots yourself."

I only backed up a step, but he smirked, so I must

have hit the right note—and the third Striker was eyeing the submachine gun. "You take most of this and get yourself fixed," he said to the first guy. "We'll come back. It costs what it costs."

"No," the first guy said, "we'll come back together. Maybe with better odds."

"I'd like to see that," Nathan said.

As the three slunk off dragging their trolley, the Warden with the submachine gun turned to Nathan.

"Is that the new policy for everyone?" she asked. "Double payment?"

"Hmmm?" Nathan said. He'd already started to drift away. "No. Just that crew. If they can afford it, we should make them pay it."

I could imagine what Trang would have to say about that. I might have averted a disaster, but only the most immediate one.

When a call came through from Georgia that evening, relayed through Pittsburgh, Janelle summoned me from my room. She left the radio area as I sat down at the transceiver, but my skin prickled at Tyler's presence across the table, the figures lingering outside the door.

"Michael wants to know how the situation's shaping up," said the voice at the other end.

It's not shaping up so much as it's falling apart, I thought, but I couldn't admit that.

"We're getting organized, proceeding as planned," I said.

I waited through the pause as he conveyed that information to Michael and got an answer. "Any additional assistance required?"

"No," I lied, feeling Tyler's gaze on me and the itch of my scabbing throat. "Everything's under control."

If I was going to have time to *get* things under control, I needed to nip this latest stirring of unrest in the bud. So the next day I wandered over to the neighborhood that had once been known as Seaton Village, peering through the darkened and mostly smashed windows of the stores along Bloor Street, a medical face mask protruding from my jacket pocket—the pocket that didn't hold my pistol. The Wardens were the only people in the city with proper masks to wear, since Michael had instructed us to hoard all the hospital supplies we could find. They served a second purpose as a visible warning to other survivors that this wasn't someone they wanted to mess with. Or, in this particular case, as a signal I wanted passed on.

I'd just turned down one of the residential streets, ambling past boxy two-story homes along a road matted with unraked autumn leaves turned mushy by the spring melt, when a car roared down the street and swerved onto the sidewalk in front of me. I flinched backward before seeing the other pulling up behind me. My hand leapt to my gun. I'd expected some sort of reception, but not one quite this aggressive.

Trang leaned out the window of the car in front of me, smiling hard. "You looking for someone, Warden?" he said.

"Yeah," I said, gathering myself. My pulse was still thudding. "I was looking for you. We need to talk."

"I'd say we need a little more than that," he said. "It's about time your boss found out exactly what kind of enemies he's making."

"No," I said quickly. "Nathan's an asshole, you won't hear me arguing against that. But your group and ours can still keep the arrangement we've had working. I told you I'm handling Nate, and I am—it's just a slow process. So I came to make a deal. You meet his new price, and I'll see the extra payments get returned to you without him knowing, until I can talk him down again. Then he's happy and you're happy, and you don't have to start some crusade that'll leave all of us hurting."

The more attention Nathan had been giving his private stash, the less he'd been checking on the public stockpile. I ought to be able to lift a few boxes and convey them over here without repercussions.

Trang made a scoffing sound. "He's got you cringing like a kicked puppy, doesn't he? *We* don't tiptoe around that kind of disrespect. And I've got an idea your own people aren't so eager to keep tiptoeing either."

He didn't say it outright, but at that moment I knew. The Strikers were making allies among the Wardens. I'd been seeing them and my colleagues as two separate issues, but if they joined forces to take Nathan down, that was two problems added up to one much bigger than the sum of their parts. Michael would lose the city completely. There was no question.

"The vaccine shipments will stop coming," I said. "Until Michael sends more people up to sort you all out, in ways I think you'll like less than mine."

"Seems like there's enough left for the rest of us," Trang said. "And Michael can try whatever he likes." He pointed a finger at me. "Listen. You didn't have to make this offer. I realize that. But whatever your way is, you're not backing it up. I'll talk to the others, and we can probably hold off a few days. If you haven't gotten Nathan sorted out 'your way' by then..." He smacked his hands together as if squashing a bug and then brushing it away.

"Right," I said, feeling sick. "Got it."

A few days. I'd already gone several without managing to budge Nathan any perceivable distance.

But it was all I had, unless I could cut off the Strikers' support on the other side.

I headed straight back to the station to track down Janelle. She was in the apparatus bay, giving orders to a few Wardens about to set off on patrol. When they'd headed out, one on a motorcycle and the others on foot, I motioned her aside.

"Tell me you're not considering throwing over Michael for these Striker idiots," I said.

The tightening of her mouth was all the answer I needed. Damn it. I hadn't realized she'd gotten *that* frustrated.

"I don't know what you're talking about," she said.

All I could do was make the same appeal I had to Trang, but at least I had her supposed loyalty and a few real successes to push on. "Michael knows what he's doing," I said. "We're getting this sorted out. It can't be done in a couple weeks. I got all of you the vaccine, didn't I? I've kept Nate from completely blowing this up. Hold off a little longer and I swear, everything will be back to normal. Better than normal, even."

"If I *did* know what you're talking about," Janelle said, "I'd ask you why the hell Michael sent that prick up here in the first place. Why he made a problem to sort out."

I couldn't answer that. If I was right, I doubted she'd appreciate being made a pawn in Michael's grand ethical experiment.

"Maybe Michael trusted Nathan," Janelle went on at

my silence. "Maybe he trusted you to keep a handle on him. You've squeaked a few things by, but you obviously don't have the nerve or the stomach to really put him down. So either way, it looks like we can't trust Michael. That's what we have to work with."

The criticism stung, more because of the truth in it. "You think *they're* any better?" I protested, but she'd stopped listening.

"You're a good kid, Drew," she said. "Stay out of the line of fire and you'll make it through."

I watched her walk away.

She was wrong about that. If everything here went to hell, Michael would make sure I paid for it, one way or another. The people here who still needed the vaccine would pay too. Maybe even Zack.

If there was no good solution, if I lost either way, I was going to have to pick the way with the fewest consequences for the people who least deserved them. Even if that meant finding the will to stomach murder. Even if I had to become someone the person I'd been a year ago would have hated.

I wasn't sure I hadn't already.

I still had my few days. I studied the other Wardens carefully, complimented people on their hard work, slipped in a comment here and there about how much Michael appreciated their efforts, and watched for signs of guilt.

How many were ready to turn? It was difficult to tell. No one let down their guard. Maybe they all saw me the way Janelle did, as a good kid who'd ultimately accomplished dick all.

Which left only Nathan.

We were down to our last dozen or so vaccine doses, which gave me a perfect opening for a chat. I found Nathan inspecting the engine of his Mercedes, the cuffs of his suit jacket rolled up and his fingertips black with grease. He'd somehow managed not to get a single smudge on his white dress shirt.

"We're getting low on the vaccine," I told him as he wiped his hands off on a rag. "I'm going to relay a message down south this afternoon, see if Michael's ready to send another batch this way."

"Approved," Nathan said. His gaze twitched to the delivery van. Its back doors were open to accept new cargo—and the space inside was empty. I stiffened. It'd been half full yesterday. Nathan must have taken the last load over to the store without me. Did he trust me even *less* now?

He turned, scanning the room. "I want to be here when it's delivered," he went on. "Can't depend on the rubes around here."

I had the feeling Nathan didn't even know what "rube" meant, only that it was an insult, but I wasn't about to correct his word usage. Especially since he might be including me under that label.

And I still had to make this last ditch attempt.

"They know not to mess with you now," I said, propping myself against the neighboring Toyota. "You've been keeping everyone on their toes."

"Hmmm," he said.

"It's been impressive watching you work, really," I said, hoping I wasn't laying it on too thick. "I didn't realize how effective it could be, never letting them know what to expect from you. No chance to get complacent."

"They can't slack off that way," Nathan said, nodding slowly, as if he'd intended it as a leadership strategy and hadn't simply been following whatever impulse hit him at any given time. "Have to pay attention."

"You know, I bet at this point you could do something generous, and it'd unsettle them even more. Make them work harder at staying on your good side."

His eyes darted back to me. "If you're trying to suggest something, spit it out."

"Me? No." I held up my hands. "Just rambling." And planting a seed. He wasn't going to take an idea directly from me—he needed to grow it himself. Give away some vaccines at half price, or free. Share some of his private stash with the other Wardens as a reward for their work. Extend a peace offering to the Strikers. All of the above. I didn't care, as long as it made them believe I'd started shifting him in the opposite direction from where he'd been headed.

"Hmmm," he said again, and then, "How's this for generous? I figure we double the vaccines we can give out when the next batch arrives."

"You want me to ask Michael for twice as much?" I said. We could probably move that many doses while they were still useable—we continued to get a small but steady stream of purchasers as people scavenged up the means to pay. I didn't see where the generosity was in that, though.

"Let him send as much as he wants," Nathan said casually. "I mean we cut what we get. Split the doses 50/50 with water. No one will know the difference. And we get twice the profit."

I stared at him, knowing my horror must be showing on my face, unable to contain it. I'd pretended to be fine with an awful lot since I'd joined the Wardens, but this... Apparently I had a hard line, and Nathan had just etched it out for me.

"The people we vaccinate will get less protection," I said. "Maybe none at all." Only they'd think they were protected, so they'd stop being so careful.

Nathan shrugged. "By the time they realize, it'll be too late for them anyway. Shame I didn't think of it before we fixed up most of the Strikers—hell, we should have given *them* straight water—but sometimes genius takes time."

He was insane. Not fickle or impulsive or even mildly unstable. Completely, irreversibly, insane. I saw it then so clearly I couldn't explain it away. Maybe he'd always been crazy under the polish of his slicked-back hair and fancy suits, or maybe getting out from under Michael's thumb had sent him spiraling, but it didn't matter now.

I slipped my hands into my pockets, fingers curling around the grip of the pistol. There was a slim possibility that shooting him might save this. Might earn me enough respect that the Wardens would follow my lead after instead of kicking me aside. But I knew from the way Janelle had spoken to me, the way the others looked at me, just how slim that chance was. And in that moment I wanted even less to bow to the standard Nathan had set, meeting violence with more violence.

"Sudden arrival of a conscience, Drew?" Nathan said.

"I want the virus gone," I said. "That only works if people are getting the full dose of the vaccine."

"Anyone stupid enough to get infected isn't worth keeping around anyway," Nathan said. "And once they're gone, the virus dies out on its own. Isn't that how it works?"

A practical angle, then. "And what do you think will happen when the 'smart' people figure out what you did?" I said. "Which they will, probably pretty quickly. What do you think they'll do to you?"

"Oh, you're worried about my safety?" He slid out his switchblade, flicking it open and closed. "I can take whatever they throw at me."

"The whole goddamned city?" I burst out. "There won't be a single person even in this station who'll stand up for you." He was building his kingdom out of kindling and lighting a flame under it—how could he not *see* that?

"There'll always be some who realize they're better off with me than against me," Nathan said. "How do you think Michael got as far as he has? The others... They can make their choices, and all that'll do is demonstrate that they never deserved my respect in the first place."

He paused, eyeing me. "Of course, now I'm wondering if you include yourself in that statement. I thought you were 'at my disposal.' Changed your mind?"

The words were a trap, laid and set. A test. Waiting for a word that would justify finishing what he'd started with that knife.

A trap. A test. The thought jiggled loose a memory:

the videos Aaron—my first boyfriend—and I had made, not far from these walls. When you had a public figure who always dodged and denied any issue, you couldn't use your own words to take them down. You had to let them provide the evidence you needed. Give them an opening—a couple guys walking around a store or into an event hand-in-hand, for example—and watch them hang themselves with their own narrow-mindedness. Then post the record online for everyone to see.

"Not at all," I made myself say. "I'm only concerned about maintaining what we have here. It's been going well, so far. But you're right; of course you can handle whatever comes up."

At the same time, my mind was spinning. I couldn't just shame Nathan, of course. If I was going to set him up for a fall, he had to fall all the way. So far he could never come back. Or the moment he recovered we'd be right back here.

Despite the surge of elation that had come with the inspiration, despite everything he'd just said, my stomach knotted. This was still a person's death I was contemplating. I'd never wanted to be responsible for that.

I'd never wanted a lot of things. I'd sure as hell never wanted to see the world brought to its knees by a deadly virus. But here we were. I was ashamed of how much I'd looked the other way before, but that didn't mean I could go right back to being the crusader I once was. It wasn't a choice between bowing to Nathan's standard and reverting to the ones I'd once held. It was in the middle ground I'd succeeded in this changed world. Trading morality against survival. I didn't have to give up my morals completely. I could still draw lines I wouldn't cross. I just had to make a few... adjustments. Find a balance between doing right and making sure I was still around to do anything at all. That was the ingenuity Michael had complimented me on.

I would be nothing but fair. I wouldn't force anything on him. I'd simply set the pieces in place, and let Nathan dictate the terms of his own destruction.

What could I use—what mattered to him? The car? I didn't have the mechanical skills to manipulate that. My gaze shifted to the delivery van, but it posed the same problem.

Nathan flipped the closed blade in his hand, brandishing it like a scepter, and I recalled my earlier thought. *A kingdom out of kindling.*

When I was fifteen, a store down the street from our house had gone up in flames. Burned to a skeleton before the firefighters could put it out. An older construction, boards and nails. "It might as well have been made of kindling," Mom had said.

I raised my chin.

"I'll put in the radio request now," I told Nathan.

"We'll squeeze everything out of this city we can get."

"That's the spirit," he said, but his smile was cold. Still, he let me walk away. Without a clue that he'd just set his own downfall into motion.

Nathan had the keys to the store's padlocks, of course, but I'd never told him I'd found the keys to the front door when I was scoping the place out. The deadbolt slid over with a thunk, and in I went. In the faint lingering sunlight of the dusk, I lugged most of the jugs and tanks of fuel into the temporary holding place I'd picked across the street. Placed the few I was leaving and several empty jugs I'd grabbed at the station at the front of the stacks so it wouldn't be immediately obvious how much was gone behind them. The guns and ammo I left where they were. If things went my way, I expected us to find better tools of negotiation.

And if they didn't, if Nathan walked away from this test, well, I was dead anyway.

I thought briefly of Kaelyn. I hadn't seen or heard any sign of her in the city since I'd arrived. Hopefully she'd made it back home to the island. I'd thought maybe I'd send someone out there to check in with her if I got things under control. I'd have liked her to know I'd at least tried. I'd have liked to explain this to Zack, too. But I couldn't exactly whip off a couple emails. I was on my own.

The contents of the last jug I splashed around the room a bit. Then I carried it outside and locked up again. I splattered more gas on the wall, the edges of the windows and the door frame, the seams in the siding where that old dry wood showed through. I stuck to the front end—I needed Nate to be able to open up the back to get inside.

Then I backed up and pulled out the box of matches I'd carried with me from Georgia. My survival gear. I struck up a flame. Watched it dance above my fingers. Inhaled the oily fumes and the tang of phosphorus, and tossed the match toward the storefront.

The flame caught, flaring as it licked up the wall. I threw another, and another. No hesitation now, just a quick swipe and a flick of the wrist. The fire crawled and leapt, wafting heat. I was lit in the darkness. My heart hammering, I spun on my heel and hurried away.

I'd just reached the corner next to the fire station when a sound like bursting popcorn carried on the air. Those boxes of ammo. The fire had already reached the back room.

I ran the rest of the way, my breath rasping by the time I burst through the entry hall.

"Where's Nathan?" I demanded of the guards. Before they could answer, Nate stepped out of the kitchen. I'd been counting on him eating dinner late, after everyone else had finished.

A few other Wardens were already standing in the common room. Tyler poked his head out of the radio area. A couple emerged from the stairwell. Our audience.

"The store," I said to Nathan. "Where you've been keeping everything. It's burning."

He froze, panic and fury twisting together on his face. "What did you do?" he said in a low, dangerous voice.

"I didn't do anything," I said, but I let my voice even out. Let him sense the challenge. Let them all sense it. For Nathan, I suspected, that would be the tipping point. Where he showed who he was at the core: a desperate, obsessive, selfish maniac.

His face was completely white now. "I'll deal with you when I have time," he promised. "For now, you're coming with me."

He grabbed my wrist as he swiveled toward the entrance to the garage. That wasn't part of the plan. I jerked my arm back automatically, and his switchblade leapt into his hand.

"Nathan," I said, loud and clear. "The whole place has gone up. You can't save anything. You'd have to be crazy to try."

It was an honest warning. I was playing fair. But Nathan, because he was insane, because fairness and honesty were concepts he didn't comprehend, took it as a dare.

"We'll see," he snapped.

I couldn't let him take me. I couldn't let there be any doubt about who made the choice, if he didn't come back. "Maybe *you* will," I said, "but I'm not going anywhere."

It was a risk. He lashed out with the knife, and I flinched away quickly enough that it only caught my cheek. Nathan took another step, and then looked toward the garage with a curse. A smoky smell was trickling in from outside.

"Don't let him leave," he ordered our spectators, and shoved past the door. In a matter of seconds, the screech of tires pierced the wall.

The guards, Janelle and Tyler, the rest of the Wardens around and trickling in at the commotion, ignored his last order and, for the moment, me. They streamed out onto the sidewalk, where the burning smell was growing thicker. A cloud of smoke obscured a swath of stars to the east. The convertible had already raced out of view. I stopped just outside the doors as the others milled about for a minute uncertainly.

Janelle made a move as if she were going to stride down the street and see what was happening. At the same moment, Nathan screamed.

I'd never heard him scream before. I'd never heard anyone scream like that, so livid amidst the pain that his fury was audible even at that distance, but we all knew it was him. It cut off with a creak and a crackling thump. Then we couldn't hear anything at all.

Janelle and a few of the others glanced back at me then. I felt the glow of the station's lights silhouetting me where I stood. I clamped down on my nausea and folded my arms over my chest. "I guess we've found out even his life didn't matter as much to him as that stuff," I said. "Unless you're on essential duties, take the night off. Things are going to look different around here tomorrow morning."

I turned and ambled to my room. I still felt sick. But at the same time inside me the kid I'd been, the crusader, lifted his arms with a rallying cry.

I surprised myself by falling asleep almost as soon as I hit the bed. When I got up and walked down to the common room the next morning, the tentative awe on the faces that looked back at me told me the first part of my job was done. I wasn't a guy who'd kill you if you got in my way; I was a guy could direct you to destroy yourself.

I didn't say anything at first, just grabbed a mug of coffee and sat down among the others. The conversation that had been carrying around the room when I'd arrived had quieted, but I still caught a few words from a woman sitting next to Tyler: "...was a *lot* of gasoline to throw away..."

I turned toward her. "It was a lot of gas," I agreed. "Why don't you and..." I picked another Warden whose expression was more uncertain than the others. "...you come with me to pick it up."

I drove us over in the delivery van, and couldn't help grinning as they blinked at the stacks of jugs I'd saved. No one else had seen Nathan's entire stash all together before now.

Before I joined them in helping load the van, I went across the street to see his store. The fire had spread to a few of the neighboring buildings, leaving a row of blackened husks. Nothing remained but crumpled edges of wall and ashes, lumps of metal and melted plastic. The entire second floor had collapsed. The scream we'd heard last night came back to me, and I swallowed thickly. He'd chosen that death, but I'd pushed him to it. That was further than I'd have preferred to go. But it was done. And it meant I could accomplish what I *did* want, for the first time since I'd come into Michael's domain.

And we are burned clean, I thought, with a vaguely religious feeling.

"Boss," the woman who'd made the gas comment said, coming up behind me, "it's not all going to fit."

Boss. For a second I wanted to laugh. Suppressing the impulse, I nodded. "We'll have to make a few trips."

I went back with her—good for them to see I didn't suddenly consider myself above a little manual labor. I left Nathan's Mercedes parked in the back alley. Anyone who wanted it, they were welcome to it.

A few of the other Wardens came over to help us unload the fuel into our storerooms at the station, exclaiming to each other at how much we'd amassed without anyone realizing it. Then I called them into the common room for my first official proclamation. I couldn't have everything I wanted all at once, but I could find a balance between the future I imagined and the power the Wardens were hungry to hold on to.

"We're knocking Nathan's gas and guns off the vaccine price," I said. "Any kids who show up under thirteen, we inoculate them for free. To compensate for Nathan's last price hike, any Strikers who show up while we still have doses left from this batch can get theirs for free too. Something Nate didn't understand is that you have to give people ways to keep living. You start crushing them, and they're going to fight. We don't *need* to fight. We've won. The city's ours. I'd like us all to stay alive and in one piece to enjoy that. Any argument?"

A couple of the Wardens chuckled and clapped their hands, and several shook their heads. The only person who spoke was Janelle.

"You'd better let Michael know what's happened."

"That's next on my list," I said.

The relay post responded a half hour later. "Tell Michael that Nathan was keeping his own hoard of supplies, and when the building caught fire, he didn't believe me that it was impossible to save anything," I said. "It looks like the ceiling came down on him. He was too wrapped up in his personal interests, and that did him in. But the rest of us are getting on just fine."

Michael's response, relayed back, was simply, "You earned it, it's yours." I wished I could have heard the tone of his voice when he'd said it. I pictured him sitting at his executive desk, hands steepled in front of him to hide a slow, satisfied smile.

I'd give it a couple weeks, so he could see my handle on things was holding, and then I'd ask about Zack and transfers.

Trang swung by that afternoon, peering around the common room as if to confirm what he'd heard was true and Nathan wasn't just hiding in a corner. "So I understand you're the man in charge now," he said, looking me up and down.

I raised my chin and met his eyes. "I am," I said. "And things are going to be different. But your people still need to remember who calls the shots."

"Let's see how it goes," he said, but his gaze strayed back to the two associates he'd brought with him, who were getting their shots without payment. The corner of his mouth turned up. We were good for now, I thought.

"Is this what you had in mind all along?" Janelle asked me later that evening, when the two of us ended up in the kitchen alone.

I laughed. "Not exactly. But you work with the means you have." The truth was, if it had really felt like a choice when Michael had proposed it, I wasn't sure I'd have taken being the boss of Toronto over staying back in Georgia with Zack, in charge of only the radio room. But the chance was in my hands: to adjust our course, to really set things right. Now that I had it, I couldn't let it go. The sense of that power, and that responsibility, thrummed through me in a way I hadn't felt in months.

This was my city, and I'd come home.

Water Song

WATER SONG

I was crossing the strait with Kaelyn, the second time I'd come back to the island since the epidemic started, when I realized it no longer felt like home.

I hadn't felt much the first time either, but then it'd been because I was so exhausted and overwhelmed by the wrenching of dread and hope inside me that I'd gone numb. This time, I looked across the bow of the motorboat I was steering, toward the pale strip of beach and the rocky shoreline that rose to the northern cliffs, and it was just another place. A place I knew, but not one I was especially attached to.

One of Mom's favorite sayings was, "A place is its people," and maybe that was why. There wasn't any uncertainty left to stir up dread or hope. I knew she and Dad were dead, and most of our neighbors, most of the kids I'd grown up with and the teachers I'd had class with, too. I knew Kaelyn and Tessa were alive. And there wasn't *anyone* on the island now. Dr. Pierce—Nell, I had to remind myself to call her now—had been talking about moving everyone to the mainland after those stir-crazy soldiers had dropped their missiles, and not long after Kaelyn and the rest of us had left with the vaccine, she and the other volunteers who'd stepped up had followed through on that. When Kaelyn and I had driven to the mainland ferry harbor, we'd found the few dozen remaining islanders squatting in a row of houses nearby. Apparently even the gang who'd been making trouble had left, heading further inland to look for easier pickings.

Kaelyn had wanted to go back, just to see—telling me she meant to go rather than asking if I'd come, I think to make it easier for me to say no. As if I would have made her go alone.

The smashed shapes of the boats clogged the island's harbor, fractured hulls protruding from the water's surface at odd angles, creeping with algae. Kaelyn had told me that the army had destroyed them in an early attempt to enforce quarantine—a wasted effort. It was hard to know what was happening anywhere other than right in front of us now, but I'd seen the news pieces, the panicked articles, in New York before the worst, and the friendly flu had already been spreading in Europe and Asia. If there were any pockets of civilization it hadn't touched, they were probably even more isolated than they'd have been before. All we had was ourselves.

I pulled the boat up to the tip of one of the docks and lashed it there, the way Dad had first taught me, not far from here, when I was a little kid: twice around the post, tail over and under and through, back and through again. In the instant I tugged it tight I had the sense of him leaning over, hand to his jaw, to inspect it.

Good work. That'll hold.

Kaelyn clambered out. It was a clear day, but windy, and her dark hair whipped around her face in spite of the scrap of cloth she'd tried to tie it back with. She reached for my hand when I joined her.

It still seemed remarkable, the sense of sureness in the way we touched each other—a statement that we were here *together*. Less than a month ago, I'd been afraid even our friendship was crumbling. I liked the way our fingers looked intertwined: almost the same shade of brown, my skin slightly lighter, hers a little bluer.

"It's so quiet," she said.

"Yeah." The wind was warbling and the waves were hissing over the broken hulls, but I knew what she meant. There was a kind of hush creeping from the vacant buildings of our town.

Hand in hand, we walked across the creaking

boards and through the harbor area to the first street. The stores and houses hadn't come through the epidemic in much better shape than the people. The missiles had turned whole blocks into masses of blackened rubble, and where they hadn't struck, the charred foundations of the buildings the gang had burned down broke up the rows. Even those buildings still standing did so limply: roofs sagging, windows shattered, doors wrenched off hinges. Here and there an entire wall had collapsed.

Shadowy impressions shifted at the edges of my vision. An impromptu dance performance I'd given on that corner, on a dare, when I was twelve. Begging my parents to stop in that burger place for their fries and gravy when I was nine, every time we passed it. My first kiss, at fourteen, under that tree at the edge of the high school's field—from a girl named Julie who'd immediately dashed back to her friends giggling, because *she'd* been dared. Little wisps of the past that teased me in the haunted emptiness of the town, as if I could have really seen those moments if I'd looked hard enough.

It was an eerie feeling, but almost familiar. All my life, the vague impression of my birth parents—back in Korea? Alive? Dead?—had peeked from behind my real mom and dad. The specter of whispered words had lingered around the doubtful looks when we went out as a family: *If you're going to adopt, why not pick a kid who'll look* right *with you? Not one everybody can't help but know?* A casual hesitation had surrounded the smiles and laughter when I pulled out a clever comment or drew the other kids into some activity, hinting that if I'd let them see the parts of me that weren't so bright or upbeat, the people who'd called themselves my friends might have drifted away with hardly a second thought. An intermittent blurring at the edges of people around me, as if I was seeing them through rippled water.

Here in the town now, with echoes caught on every surface, the whole world might as well have been underwater. There was a new depth to it, too—a distance between me and the memories, as if all that had happened to some other guy. In a lot of ways, I guessed it had.

Kaelyn's fingers squeezed mine as we approached her uncle's house, where she and I, and Tessa and Meredith and Gav, had been living before. More ghosts waited for *her* there than anywhere else.

She sucked in a breath and pushed open the door, which had been hanging ajar. The bag of ferret food I'd left out lay empty and gnawed in the middle of the kitchen floor. "Mowat!" Kaelyn called. "Fossey!"

No scamper of tiny feet came running. She bit her lip, considering the back door, which was swinging in the wind.

"They could have gotten out," she said.

"I'm sure they did." I doubted there'd been enough food in here to last them the months we'd been gone. "They were smarter than a pretty large number of people I've known. They've probably been living it up with the whole town to themselves."

She smiled with only half her mouth. "Pets don't usually do so well out in the wild."

A joke popped into my head about how far from wild the town was, but she didn't look as if that was what she needed. I let go of her hand to put my arms around her, hugging her to me. "You can't save everyone," I said.

"I know." She leaned her face against me for a moment, brushed a kiss to my shoulder, then straightened up.

We meandered through the house, Kaelyn grabbing plastic bags that she filled as we went. Mostly with things for Meredith—games and clothes, and the arts and crafts stuff Meredith was still so enthusiastic about —but some for her too. A couple framed photos of her family, a few notebooks labeled with her narrow handwriting. A dress I'd never seen her wear—maybe she'd bought it after I'd left for New York—and a sweater I could tell her grandmother had knitted. Two pairs of jeans, scuffed up sneakers. A burned DVD she paused over, lips twisting, before shoving it in with the rest. Maybe someday we'd be using computers again.

The backpack stuffed with the few things I'd taken from my house, back when I'd first returned and moved in here, was slumped near the couch. I picked it up, not sure how much I still wanted the contents but figuring I might as well bring it, while Kaelyn poked through the kitchen again. Nell had told us that she and the others had gathered all the practicalities they could find—food, medical supplies, fuel—before they'd moved, so it wasn't a surprise when Kaelyn came over to the living room empty-handed.

The air mattress Gav had been sleeping on was a sunken mass in the middle of the rug. Kaelyn looked at it, and her jaw tightened. My stomach tightened with it.

My comment from earlier came back to me: *You can't save everyone.* I had the feeling she was remembering it too, and I wished I hadn't said it. She was the one clear thing I had in this underwater world. Just herself, my best friend, my girlfriend, no shadows bleeding around her as she turned and reached for the bags she'd left by the door. The one part of my life that still belonged to me from before killer viruses and murderous gangs and all that those had driven us to.

"Let's go," she said.

Our eyes met, and I had to wonder what specters she saw when she looked at *me*.

*   *   *

Meredith squealed as she dug through the bags—"You remembered my favorite skirt! And the markers with the scents!"—forgetting to pout about being left out of the trip. "Did you bring Mowat and Fossey?" she asked when she was finished. "Where are they?"

"I don't know," Kaelyn admitted. "They had to leave the house to find more food while we were away. They probably wouldn't want to go back in their cage now."

"Oh," Meredith said. A hint of the pout came back.

"Why don't we take those markers and some paper over to see if Dorrie's kids want to try them out?" I suggested.

When she hesitated, touching the box fondly, Kaelyn added, "We'll be able to find more if those get used up, Mere, I promise. You know how much those kids could use a distraction."

"Of course," Meredith said, lifting her chin. The steely determination that came into her eyes was something new since we'd picked her up at the artists' colony, at least as far as I could remember. A determination to show how mature she could be, it usually seemed, which had its advantages but also didn't look quite right on her seven-year-old face. She snatched up the box and a sheaf of paper.

Outside, the two women who'd taken over the house next door were standing on their porch, discussing whether it was warm enough to try planting anything in the yard. Howard was ambling along the sidewalk with a couple of the older guys, taking in the spring air. Some of the orphaned kids Dorrie and her brother Mason looked after were sitting out on their lawn, nudging toys around or just sprawling, watching their surroundings. As we headed over I saw Mason call back one of the smaller ones who had wandered off the grass. I didn't see why they couldn't roam a little more —this street, at least, was safe enough—but I guessed it was easier to keep track of them by keeping them close.

After all, while there was more life here than in the town across the strait, this place was haunted in different ways. If you looked for them, you'd notice the figures positioned on the front steps of a house at either end of the block, hunting rifles across their knees, ready to defend the little we had if they needed to. And when the wind blew a speckling of dirt into our faces and Meredith coughed, everyone's head jerked around, every body tensing, until they saw it was okay after all.

Nell had mentioned that the last of the infected islanders had died a month ago and no one had gotten sick since then, but we all knew that didn't make those who weren't vaccinated like I was, or who hadn't survived the virus like Meredith had, truly protected. We didn't know how long the virus might linger on any surface. We didn't know that an infected person from outside this little enclave wouldn't wander our way.

When Dorrie came out of the house, she asked Kaelyn, "So they didn't say when they'll get the vaccine out this way?" as if Kaelyn hadn't already answered that question a dozen times since we'd arrived here. As if the people who'd asked wouldn't have passed on her answer. Everyone wanted to confirm it directly with the source.

"No," Kaelyn said, her smile slanting. "But it'll probably be a while. They'll cover the more populated places first."

Assuming that, between the Wardens and the CDC, they had enough raw materials to keep making the vaccine that long. Assuming Michael kept up his end of the deal and the Wardens didn't start fighting with the doctors at the CDC again. Maybe if we'd waited a month or two longer they'd have been producing enough for us to take a batch back here with us, but Kaelyn had already been worried about how Meredith would be coping. We hadn't known whether she and Tessa were even still alive.

So now we did whatever else we could to pitch in. We went out with the scavenging parties, methodically making our way through the streets to the west. We washed or wiped down every item we carried back. We brought Meredith over to play with the orphaned kids, who seemed standoffish with her—whether because of her long absence from the island or because they envied the family in Kaelyn she had to go back to afterward, I wasn't sure. We helped round everyone up to present ourselves to Nell every evening so she could take our temperature and test our reflexes. "Just a precaution," she said to Kaelyn. Still, when I stopped outside a house a bunch of us were about to search and scratched the side of my neck, everyone froze, staring, until I held up my hand and said, "It's okay, just a regular itch!" And even then I saw them eyeing me, making sure I didn't continue, for several minutes after.

Nothing felt like progress, only treading water. Less than three weeks after we'd arrived, Kaelyn asked me to go for a walk with her. We wandered down to the harbor and sat at the end of the dock where we'd huddled a few months ago, watching the island burn. Kaelyn stared across at it, the distant slice of land hovering over the water of the strait. I wasn't surprised when she said, "I can't stay here."

As soon as Kaelyn mentioned it, it seemed almost all of the islanders had been thinking about leaving. In ten days we put together a caravan of the largest vehicles we could find and all the supplies we could reasonably carry. Altogether there were forty-three of us that set off early one morning for Toronto. Kaelyn figured that city was the first place in our end of the country the vaccine was likely to get to, considering the extent of Michael's presence there, and it was one she and I were at least somewhat familiar with.

Now that we knew there was no one still holding people up at the border, we planned a shorter route than the one we'd taken in January, this time cutting through Maine. With the roads clear of snow, we expected to make the trip that'd taken us nearly two weeks that winter in just a day and a half.

We stopped in the evening in the first town we came to after crossing into Ontario. The residential neighborhood appeared to be deserted, but Kaelyn and I had learned our lesson the last time. Several of the adults stayed behind with the kids, the vehicles, and an assortment of weapons while the rest of us split up into groups of five to check the abandoned homes and cars nearby for anything worth scavenging.

Kaelyn led her group off to the south, and I headed north with mine. My thoughts drifted after her as we tried the doors of various houses and siphoned gas from a gray sedan. We'd made sure someone in each of the groups had a gun. I was carrying the .38 we'd lifted from the Wardens who'd come after us before, the ones Justin and Tobias had shot, in the back pocket of my cargo pants. Kaelyn still had the service pistol Tobias had left behind. The difference was, Dad had insisted I become a decent shot and as far as I knew Kaelyn had never fired a gun. I'd walked her through the basics, but we didn't have bullets to spare for real training. If her group ran into trouble...

"Leo," Howard said as he screwed the cap on the jug of gas, "you think we should keep going?"

I yanked my thoughts back to the task at hand. I was supposed to be protecting *these* people from trouble.

"Let's do another block," I said, scanning the street. Still no sign of anyone living here, but we hadn't had any idea the guy who'd infected Gav was around until he'd been right there charging up the driveway at us.

It was hard to keep my thoughts from looping like that, back to Kaelyn, to what we'd been through together, what she might be facing now. Howard and the others were looking to me as some sort of leader—because I had the gun? Because I'd traveled across the country more than once?—but I really wasn't one. I'd been following Kaelyn since we set off that first time with the vaccine. That'd been her mission, just like this was. I believed we were doing the right thing, moving everyone to the city, but if I thought about it honestly, I was here because she'd wanted to go. If she'd wanted to stay by the island, I wouldn't have argued.

I could still remember, too clearly, the agony in her voice when she'd noticed I wasn't entirely comfortable with some of the more cutthroat decisions she'd made on the way to Atlanta. When she'd told me that she couldn't shoulder the responsibility for what I did, what

I believed in. I didn't expect her to. But what could I really contribute that wasn't just helping someone else? The only mission I'd ever had before was becoming respected enough for my dancing to make a career out of it. There wasn't much point in trying to pursue *that* in a world where "career" was hardly a thing—and it wasn't as if dancing was going to help anyone survive.

My whole life before had been about performing in one way or another, really. Entertaining people. Mainly because that had seemed like the only remotely special thing I had to offer. Which meant there wasn't much I could do that mattered now, was there?

That thought ate at me as we started along the next street over, but I didn't know how to start dealing with it. As long as I stayed alive and Kaelyn stayed alive, how could I complain? So I focused on the first part of that, eyes alert and ears perked.

We managed to fill most of our bags with canned goods from a couple of the houses on that block. I was about to suggest it was time to head back as we stepped out of the bungalow on the corner, when a distant shriek made the words snag in my throat.

I stiffened, reaching for the pistol. The sound had come from north of us, the opposite direction from where the rest of our group was, so it shouldn't be anyone we knew. My companions exchanged looks, Howard frowning. Like me, he was safe—relatively—if it was someone with the flu, since he was one of the few who'd had it and recovered, but the others weren't.

Of course, it might not be someone sick. It might be someone who could use our help. I shifted my weight from one foot to the other, and glanced at Howard.

"We should take a quick look," I said, and, to the others, "Stay close, but let the two of us go first."

I half expected someone to argue, but they nodded and followed my lead.

We stole through the long shadows of the houses toward the noise. The shriek had cut off, but as we crept closer I distinguished what I thought were two different voices, one pleading and the other sobbing. It could be both someone sick and someone else who needed help.

As we turned the corner, the voices became clearer. "Just let me out, sweetheart," the first was calling out. "You need to open the door. Your mommy can't look after you when she's shut away like this. You *need* me."

The sobbing broke off briefly as a boy shouted, "I can't! I can't, I can't, I can't!"

I spotted him, a small, pale figure cowering by an open second-story window in the house one over from the corner, and sped up to a jog. He glanced out just as I reached the house, and stared down at me, his cheeks shiny with tears. He looked about Meredith's age, maybe a bit older—seven or eight.

"What's going on?" I asked, checking him for signs

of infection. His eyes were red-rimmed, but that was probably from the crying. As he continued staring at me dumbly, he didn't scratch or sneeze or cough. The other voice had fallen silent, but I thought I heard the rattle of a door in its frame.

"What do you need?" I tried again.

He didn't answer.

"Cody!" the woman's voice yelled, and he flinched away from the window. "Please, sweetheart, please!" A childish wail split the air. I couldn't tell who'd made it.

"I don't think the kid's sick," I said to the others. "And it looks like he's alone, other than..."

The door was rattling again, louder, followed by a volley of coughs. My skin prickled. *Someone* was sick up there.

The boy didn't return to the window, and my companions didn't move. Well, to be careful, it was better I handled this anyway. "I'm going inside," I said. Without giving myself a chance to rethink it, I headed to the front door. It opened at my push and I hurried up the stairs.

The boy must have heard me coming. He was standing in a doorway when I reached the second floor hallway, framed by the hazy glow of the setting sun through the window I'd first seen him at. His bedroom, I guessed from the bit of furniture I could see. His blond hair was tangled, his face sallow.

A door at the opposite end of the hall was the one rattling. "Cody!" the woman cried, and it shuddered. "Talk to me! Open it up! I need to see you!"

"Your mom?" I said quietly.

The boy inclined his head, his body rigid. I took another step toward him.

"She locked herself in that room?"

Another incline.

"You don't know how to let her out?"

Another.

I could imagine what might have happened. She'd realized she was sick, and shut herself away from him so she wouldn't infect him. Maybe the door was locked with a key and she'd tossed it somewhere neither of them could reach. Maybe she'd gone as far as nailing it shut and throwing away any tools she could have used to pry it open. There were a lot of ways she could have made her situation permanent. Made the room beyond that door into a coffin.

My stomach knotted. We couldn't help her, any more than we'd been able to help Gav or Tobias. Even if we figured out a way to get to her, Nell didn't have the equipment here to attempt a blood transfusion, the only treatment that had worked for anyone, and letting this woman out would put nearly every one of the islanders at risk. Not to mention the son she'd been so determined to save.

We *could* help her do that.

"She's got the friendly flu," I said. "There's nothing we can do for her. I'm so sorry—I wish there was."

He nodded, and I wondered how many deaths he'd already witnessed in the last few months. His dad's? A sibling's? The images of Gav's body surrounded by the papers he'd torn up during his hallucinations, of following Tobias's footprints through the snow in vain, passed through my mind, and I swallowed hard.

"You can stay with her, if you want," I told him, "but you can also come with us. We're only here for one night. There are a bunch of us—kids, your age—and we'd look after you. I know it's awful to think about leaving her, but... if you stay here, soon you'll be alone."

He looked at me with those desperate eyes. I held out my hand. "They'll be making dinner right now," I added. "How long has it been since you ate?"

His hand lifted to his belly, and his mouth worked. He peeked at the locked door. His mother screeched, and he winced, fresh tears trickling out—and I decided I wasn't giving him a choice.

"Come on," I said, as gently as I could, and took him by the elbow. I was prepared to scoop him up and carry him away, but he let me tug him toward the stairs, and down, and out to the sidewalk where the other four were waiting. He balked there, turning around. His mom was pounding on the door now, shouting his name.

She'd never know he was gone. She'd keep calling out to the echo of him she'd sense beyond the door, until her voice gave out.

"This is what she'd have wanted," I said. "She locked herself in there so you could keep living. I promise you, if she could stop being sick for a minute, she'd tell you to go."

He lowered his head, and walked with us back to the caravan.

Kaelyn poured over a map of Toronto during the morning's drive, but it wasn't until she finished directing me, at the head of our caravan, to the section of the city where she wanted us to stop that I found out what she'd been looking for. We parked on the street in front of a wide brick building—a dance studio. Kaelyn was grinning.

"I figured we'll actually *live* in that condo building," she said, pointing to a five-story building in yellow stucco half a block away. "But I thought you'd appreciate this being so close."

We had nothing, really, and somehow she'd managed to give me the most enormous gift. She looked so pleased I had to kiss her. Meredith kicked the back of my seat.

"You can make out later," she said. "I want to see

where we're going to stay."

A bunch of us inspected all the buildings within two blocks first, to make sure no one else was squatting nearby, and then we moved into the condos. It turned out to be an ideal set-up: just two entrances, one through the lobby that we could easily guard, and a back door we immediately barricaded. The social room in the basement with adjacent kitchen gave us a place where we'd be able to cook and eat communal meals once Howard got one of the generators we'd hauled with us hooked up to the electrical system. Someone had looted the place already, breaking the locks on the condo doors and carting off most of their contents, but that made it easier for us to move in without feeling like we were displacing the real owners. With twenty-eight apartments in all, we had lots of space to spread out in.

We spent the rest of the day wiping down every surface in the building with hospital-grade disinfectant, which might not be enough to kill the virus if it had lingered somewhere but was the best we could do. The next morning, though, Kaelyn and I checked out the studio.

The lock on its door was broken too. Light spilled across the wooden floor from the large front window. One wall held a ballet barre in front of a row of mirrors, the others blank except for a small bulletin board with a few audition postings and performance announcements tacked to it.

I kicked off my shoes automatically and padded on my socked feet into the middle of the space. The floor was smooth and firm beneath me, but with the spring all good dance floors had. I'd never had a surface this good to practice on until those couple months in New York City before the world went to hell. I bobbed up and down on my feet, and then pushed off into a couple pirouettes. Sloppy—I hadn't warmed up, and these weren't the best clothes for dancing—but satisfying in a way I'd missed.

"What do you think?" Kaelyn asked.

"It's perfect." I looked over at her where she'd stopped not far from the door to give me room, at the light in her eyes as she smiled at my approval, and a swell of affection rushed up through me. I walked back to her, cupped her face, leaned close.

"Have I mentioned recently that I love you?" I said.

Her smile widened. "I'm totally okay with you mentioning it again."

I kissed her, gently, and then, as her fingers curled against the back of my neck, more intensely. My heart thumped faster than I could blame on the pirouettes.

Of course, we weren't really alone. The door's hinges sighed as it opened, and Mason peered in.

"Ah," he said, looking awkward, as Kaelyn and I stepped apart. "Kaelyn, Nell wants to talk to you."

"Sure," Kaelyn said. She gave me another smile, one that promised *Later*, and headed out.

After she'd gone, I sat and stretched in deep slow movements, both warming up and cooling off, absorbing the feel of the space. "Think of your stage as a participant in the dance," one of our instructions at the academy had liked to say. "The better you know it, the better you can partner it." I stripped off my socks when I stood up again, and was tempted to kick off my jeans too, but Mason had shown how easily I could be interrupted and I wasn't keen to have someone walk in on me in my boxers.

When I was limber enough, I tested out a short section of choreo we'd been working on in jazz class right before I'd taken off for home. I didn't know how much longer the school had stayed open after that. There'd already been a few people sick when I left, and many more throughout the city. Most of them, the students I'd danced alongside, the teachers who'd led us, would be dead now.

In a distant part of my mind, I could hear the instructor counting off the beats, see figures reaching and turning in the edges of my vision. My footfalls echoed through the empty room, and I halted. My throat had tightened.

Dancing used to be my one clear thing—the one act that felt true, all the way down. I was meant for it and it was meant for me, nothing there to doubt. Even more so after Kaelyn had moved away when we were eleven, leaving me with all those island-born kids who couldn't help seeing me as an outsider no matter how much they enjoyed my company.

But dancing had its own shadows now. I could still do it, obviously—I still loved it—I couldn't imagine giving it up. It just didn't make a difference to anyone except me. And that hollowed it even for me, knowing there was no one to dance with, no one to dance for, not the way there used to be.

I *wanted* to be doing things that made this world better... not worse, like some of what I'd had to do before to make it this far. If this was all I had, all I could offer that couldn't have been filled in by any person who happened to be around, then my being alive and here meant pretty much nothing.

I was doing some good, I reminded myself. I'd saved a kid from an angry bear in that town in Georgia. I'd made sure Cody would have a chance at a life.

I put my socks and shoes back on, and headed up the street to see what else needed to be done at the condo building. I was almost there when a silver sports car turned the corner up ahead and cruised toward me.

I froze, my nerves prickling with the urge to run. Anyone driving around that casually was almost definitely a Warden. Our group had parked all our vehicles in the building's small underground garage, but there were other signs of our occupation: voices carrying through open windows, the sheets we'd been boiling draped over balcony railings, garbage bags full of the previous inhabitants' personal effects, which no one wanted staring at them, lined up on the front lawn to be hauled elsewhere later that day. I glanced at the nearest driveway, but whoever was in the car had to have already seen me. If they were going to make trouble, the others might need me—or at least my pistol.

The car slowed as it passed the condo building, and I made out a woman's face behind the reflections on the windshield. She came to a stop beside me, pulling a surgical mask up over her mouth and nose.

"New in town?" she said.

"Yes," I said, "but we know Michael makes the rules here. We're not going to get in your way."

If she was surprised that I knew the score, her eyes didn't show it. "How many of you and where are you from?"

"About forty—ten just kids—and Nova Scotia." I wasn't sure what she might make of that information. Remembering the Wardens Kaelyn and I had encountered on our way from Atlanta, the way they'd backed off when they'd recognized who we were, I added, "Kaelyn Weber's here with us. Whoever's running things, they should mention that to Michael before you decide anything about us."

"Keep to yourselves and contribute if we ask you to, and we shouldn't need to make any decisions," she said, and drove off.

I mentioned the incident to Kaelyn and Nell, and we posted an extra guard by the front door for the next few days, but no one else came by while we were finishing settling in. Then, just as a group of us were setting off to explore the commercial strip to the east, a motorcycle growled down the street and stopped in front of the building.

"I heard I can find Kaelyn Weber here," the driver said as he took off his helmet.

"Drew!" Kaelyn cried, and launched herself at her brother. He hugged her, laughing, and the other islanders gathered closer with a flurry of questions.

"I would have come sooner," Drew said. "But things have been a little... complicated."

"Is everything okay, with us being here?" I asked. "The Wardens in charge don't have a problem with us?"

"Well, ah, it turns out I'm kind of the one in charge," he said, scratching the back of his head.

Kaelyn's eyebrows rose. "How did *that* happen?"

"It's a long story," he said, in a tone that made me guess it wasn't a completely pleasant one. "I'll tell you later. I can't stick around too long right now. I just wanted to give you an official welcome. What are you all doing here?"

"We wanted everyone to get the vaccine as soon as possible," Kaelyn said. "Has any made it up here yet?"

He nodded. "We've gone through a couple batches already—should have another coming in a week or two. I've been encouraging Michael to negotiate another deal with the CDC, so they can send one of their people with our portion and some of their own, with the understanding we'll let them take care of the kids and the elderly and people like that for free. Still working on the trust issue with them, understandably. But I'll make sure everyone here who needs it gets the shot without payment. Just be careful until then. We're still seeing newly infected people; the friendly flu's not beaten yet."

It would have been hard to forget how precarious life still was. When we finally did set off for the commercial strip, we came across a man's corpse sprawled in the middle of the road. From the contorted angle of his body, he might have been hit by a car, but there was no way of knowing if he'd been infected too.

"Should we just leave him?" one of the guys said, covering his mouth with his hand, when we'd stopped several feet away.

"It'll be more of a health hazard the longer we leave it, if we're going to keep coming this way," Nell said.

So it was up to Kaelyn, Howard, a woman named

Liz who'd also survived the virus, and me to move it. I kept my eyes averted, breathing through the cloth I'd tied over my mouth as we wrapped the body in several layers of garbage bags, but I couldn't completely avoid the sight of gnawed flesh or the putrid stink. Long after we'd carted the corpse to the nearest graveyard, which seemed like the most reasonable place to leave it, and I'd scrubbed myself with antiseptic soap and scalding water, the memory would flicker up with a sourness in the back of my mouth, making my stomach churn.

There'd be more—in and around the hospitals especially, but we'd stumbled on other bodies in random places when we'd been in the city in the winter. As it got warmer, something would have to be done about them, or the smell... I got queasy just thinking about it. Maybe Drew could get the Wardens organized and truck the corpses out to the mass graves that had been created before the infrastructure here had fallen apart. Leaving them would be as unpleasant and unsanitary for them as it'd be for us.

There was, at least, no sign of the friendly flu within our group. Not long after Drew's visit, Cody came down to dinner with the other kids into the dining room we'd set up in the basement.

"He must be glad to be out," I said to Kaelyn. Nell had made one of the condos into a quarantine area, and Cody had been isolated there, to make sure he hadn't picked up his mom's infection, for the last two weeks. I'd tried to visit him a few times, figuring he had to be lonely, but Dorrie had shooed me off, saying he wasn't in a good mood for company. I knew that when Meredith had been allowed in to try to play with him, he'd refused to talk to her, and he'd hit Howard the first day here. I couldn't blame him for acting out a little. He'd obviously been through a lot, and now he was stuck among strangers.

"Maybe he'll open up now that he doesn't have to worry that he's sick," Kaelyn said.

We studied him for a moment. Cody didn't look as though he was opening up. He was sitting between the two nine-year-olds, Owen and Mya, who were sniping at each other past him as if he were a statue and not a fellow kid, while he jabbed at his plate. Dorrie walked by and leaned over to say something to him, and he shook his head with a jerk.

"Has he talked to anyone so far?" I asked. He *could* speak—*I can't, I can't, I can't,* he'd wailed at his mom— and I'd assumed his silence with me afterward had been out of shock.

"I don't think so," Kaelyn said. "I guess he needs a little more time. Dorrie takes good care of them."

"She does," I agreed, but I kept watching Cody. As Dorrie walked away, he bowed his head over his plate, shoulders hunched as if to shield himself—or to warn people away from him. The posture gave me an ache of recognition. Not long ago, I'd felt like that: lost and adrift, focusing all my energy on holding my pain and regrets inside. The pain and regrets about the people I'd lost, but also the people I'd purposely left behind. The roommate whose wallet I'd grabbed to get bus fare to the border, the sick woman whose car I'd stolen after she offered me a ride. The people whose stuff I'd taken off with when I'd run from the border camp. Remembering that raw, desperate time still made me twist up inside.

Cody hadn't really had a choice, with his mom— there wasn't any way he could have done better by her. But it was his *mom* he'd left to die. I could only imagine how much the guilt might be eating him up.

I'd needed to let those feelings out, to admit to Kaelyn the horrors I'd seen and done to make it back to the island, before I'd been able to start recovering. Maybe Cody needed that too, before he'd really feel he belonged here. I'd brought him with us, but I hadn't brought him all the way in. And there might not be anyone else here who could come close to understanding where he was coming from. I'd stood there with him listening to her rattle the door and call out his name.

* * *

The next day, I stopped by the penthouse suites where

all the kids except Meredith were rooming. Dorrie spent the nights with the girls in one and Mason with the boys in the other, and they'd turned both of the open concept living spaces into playrooms which the whole group alternated between. Today they were gathered on the girls' side. Meredith had come with me, and she bounded straight to the dress-up box to paw through the clothes there.

Her energy seemed out of sync with the rest of the room. Only the two toddlers, who were stacking blocks and then smashing their towers, looked as if they were enjoying themselves. Paulette, the eleven year old who was the oldest of the group, was curled up in a chair with a magazine, but her gaze kept drifting away from it. Owen and Mya perched at the marble kitchen island with pencil crayons and paper, their drawings aimless doodles, their expressions bored. A couple of the younger kids were putting together a puzzle at the rate of about one piece a minute, and another was pushing a toy dump truck around himself in the same steady circle, over and over. Cody lay on the sofa, scowling at the ceiling. The only sounds in the room other than Meredith's rustling through the box were the rattling of the toddlers' blocks and a muted yelp as Mya poked Owen in the side.

I'd noticed the kids seemed a little lethargic before, but I hadn't spent much time around the whole group since we'd moved in here. "Are they normally this quiet?" I said to Dorrie.

She gave me a little smile. "This is pretty typical. I was hoping the move would do them good, help them start to move on, but I have to wonder if leaving the island didn't just make them more aware of what they've lost. We do our best to distract them, but..." She shrugged. "You can't hurry healing."

"I can try to help with the distraction part," I offered. I'd meant to reach out to just Cody, but a group activity could work just as well. Singling him out might have been too much pressure to start with anyway, and the rest of the kids did look as though they could use *something*.

I wandered farther into the room, searching for inspiration. I'd had a knack for this as a kid, coming up with some unexpected idea and getting everyone around me caught up in it—playing ringmaster. It had been fun, exhilarating, and deep down I think I'd been aware that if I was leading I couldn't get left out.

Cody didn't look in the mood for anything too wild. I picked up a Snakes and Ladders game and carried it to the kid-sized table and chairs in the middle of the living room. As I opened the box, Cody glanced over and turned away again.

"Hey," I said. "I need someone to play with."

He rolled onto his side to face me, his scowl relaxing

a sliver, but he didn't get up. Owen peered at us from his stool.

"Snakes and Ladders is boring," he declared.

"Well, it's a good thing we're going to play Lakes and Snadders, then," I said.

He frowned, and Mya ambled over. "How do you play Lakes and Snadders?"

"I'll show you if you can get two more people playing," I said.

She marched to the sofa. "Come on, Cody," she said. He grimaced at her and she put her hands on her hips. With a sigh that sounded far too old for him, he got up and plopped into one of the four chairs. The boy who'd been pushing the dump truck came over, wide-eyed, and took another. Meredith appeared by my shoulder as Mya sat down in the last.

"Can I play too?" she asked.

"There's just four pieces," Mya informed her before I could answer. Meredith's eyebrows drew together, but she stayed standing beside me. Owen drifted over too, and even Paulette perked up behind her magazine.

"We can always do another game after," I said, and tapped the board. "The rules of Lakes and Snadders are, every time you take a turn, you get to make up a new rule, and we all have to remember all of them. The rule can be anything you want, as long as people can do it at the table."

"Like, you go up the snakes instead of down?" the little boy asked.

"We can get crazier than that," I said, and then my mind went blank. It shouldn't be that hard to think of something they'd find amusing. "You could say... anyone who lands on a blue square has to sing a song, or something like that."

The boy grinned, and Mya leaned forward intently.

"Cody can't play then," Owen said. "He won't say what his rules are."

Cody aimed his scowl at Owen, and Owen smirked. Then Meredith said, "I can help Cody—I'll give him ideas and he can pick which one. He doesn't have to talk for that."

"Good thinking," I said gratefully. Cody eyed her as she knelt beside him, but he didn't make any gesture of protest.

"I'll go first," Mya announced, grabbing the dice. "My first rule is, if your name starts with M, you get to roll twice."

When it was Cody's turn, Meredith whispered in his ear. He shook his head at her first two suggestions, and nodded for the third: "If you land on a red square you get to go again," she said for him. I used my singing idea since I hadn't come up with a better one. The little boy decided we would all go down ladders instead of up. And so it went. Mya looked triumphant when she came up with the rule that you could move someone else backward the same number of spaces you moved forward, and then less happy when the very next turn Cody sent *her* back, to the top of a ladder she then had to go down. I tried to mitigate the growing tension by saying the same person couldn't be sent backward twice in a row, but they still ended up in a duel between the two of them, focusing on who could make things worse for the other.

The younger boy started to get confused. The fifth time around, Cody had shaken his head to six or seven of Meredith's ideas when Owen, who was still watching, rolled his eyes and said, "This is so dumb."

Cody looked at him, and then reached out and shoved the board. It slid to the edge of the table, the pieces skidding off onto the floor. He stood up and raised his hands in a victory pose. Owen snorted disdainfully, but when Mya started laughing, he laughed too. And that was the only time Cody smiled.

There didn't seem to be much point in trying to salvage the game. As Meredith helped me gather the pieces, Mya dragged Cody over to the pencil crayons. Dorrie stepped in when they started scribbling right on the countertop, and they and Owen went off to huddle in the corner by the gas fireplace. Cody still hadn't said a word. His gaze flicked back and forth between his companions as they alternately plotted and sparred, with that same defensive curl to his shoulders.

I didn't think they were going to be the most comforting company, but getting him comfortable with me was obviously going to require a different approach.

"He's *always* with them now," I complained to Kaelyn a few days later as we meandered along the boardwalk at the edge of the beach just south of the condo building. "If I try to take him aside, or to talk to all of them, he acts like I'm not there, and Mya or Owen will tell me, 'We're *busy*.'" I imitated their offended tone.

"At least he's made friends?" Kaelyn offered. We glanced over to where the kids were playing in the sand on this rare trip outside the safety of the condo building. A bunch of us had combed the beach for bodies or other hazards before Dorrie had agreed to Meredith's suggestion that they all trek over here.

The kids did look a little more animated than before, in the sunlight, but Owen and Mya tended to take their animation in less-than-constructive directions. Mason was just chiding Owen for kicking down one of the little kids' lopsided sandcastles while Owen glowered at him. Mya and Cody stood together watching, Mya snickering and Cody wearing his usual dark expression.

"I guess," I said. "But he doesn't look any happier hanging out with them. The way they talk to everyone, they might be making him feel *worse*."

I guessed for all I knew Cody might have been a bully himself in his life before. But I hadn't seen him do much besides tag along with the other two and watch their exploits looking sullen, as though he didn't exactly enjoy being there but he was afraid there wasn't anywhere else to go. Afraid he didn't deserve kindness?

Meredith ran up to us with Paulette and the little girl who'd lost her sandcastle in tow. "Can we go swimming?" she asked, waving toward the lake, which stretched away from the curve of the beach as far as I could see. Lake Ontario looked as vast as the ocean from here, but, at the same time, disorientingly different—the waves only big enough to sputter, not crash, as they rolled in, no salt in the vaguely fishy breeze drifting off them.

It was hot for May, the sun intense overhead, but Kaelyn hesitated. "My parents told us not to go in the water," she said. "It's not that clean near the city—the runoff from the sewage system... But, you know, that hasn't been operating for a while. It should be better now. Even before, some people still swam here."

Dorrie must have overheard, because she joined us, saying, "I don't think we should risk it, even so. Sorry, kids. It'll be hard to keep you all together in the water too. We're better up here."

"Awww," Meredith groaned, but when none of us

budged she plopped down on the edge of the boardwalk near the others. She and Paulette started sketching figures with a stick in the sand, Meredith chattering about the intricacies of the outfit she was designing while Paulette mostly just nodded.

Kaelyn and I ambled on, staying on the boardwalk as it veered toward a peninsula dotted with trees.

"It's not just Cody," I said, still turning over the problem. "All the kids, you can tell they're struggling—even Owen and Mya, that's probably part of the reason they act like the way they do—but how do you help a five year old cope with the idea that he's never going to see his parents again?"

"How did you move past the things you'd been through?" Kaelyn said.

I considered. "By talking about them, but that's where I'm getting stuck with Cody. And... I guess by actually moving, when I let myself start dancing again. It was a way to channel the feelings into something else, something better."

"Maybe that would help them too. Not real dancing, but acting out their grief. Giving them something to literally throw themselves into."

"Yeah," I said. I could try it. I couldn't see making any *less* progress than I'd made so far, which was basically none. In fact, I might have been moving backwards.

As that thought crossed my mind, Kaelyn glanced toward the lake, suddenly pensive, and I remembered a time I had literally moved backwards. A moment I'd relieved dozens of times in the last two months: when we'd been standing in that snowy driveway, checking out the abandoned pick-up truck, and the infected guy had come running at us.

I'd stepped back, like everyone else. Everyone except Gav, who'd rushed forward to protect the cold box and the vaccine inside it.

It should have been me. I should have gotten in there, stopped the guy—after all, I'd been protected and Gav hadn't. But I hadn't known that for sure, the vaccine had been untested, and my body had reacted on instinct, away from the threat.

If I'd been more brave—more dedicated, more selfless—maybe Gav would still be alive.

That regret niggled deeper than any other, because it wasn't just regret. Because I knew there was a part of me that would have hesitated to wish it different.

The boardwalk ended, and we wandered onto a path that wound around and through the peninsula's sparse forest. With the breeze rustling the trees and the buildings hidden from view, it felt as though we'd left the city far behind. We paused by a rocky bit of shore. Kaelyn took my hand. And I found myself saying, "How do you think things would be, if Gav hadn't..."

Seeing the shadow of pain crossing her face, I couldn't finish the question. It was complete enough anyway.

"Why are you thinking about that?" she said.

"I don't know," I said. "I'm sorry. Forget it."

As if either of us could. She nudged a pebble with the toe of her sneaker, and I waited, braced for what she might say. I'd started to think maybe she wasn't going to say anything after all when she dragged in a breath.

"The thing is, it's impossible to know, isn't it? There are so many other things that could have happened differently if he'd still been with us, the rest of the way to Atlanta. And those things would have changed him, and us. It's not like I haven't wondered about it. But when I try to picture it, even just heading down to the States with him, it's... blurry."

"Yeah," I said, and something inside me closed up around a little jab of hurt, even though I couldn't imagine what good answer she could have given me.

"Leo." She tugged my hand so I turned to face her. "The one thing I do know," she said, "is if you'd come back to the island, and I hadn't been with him, and you hadn't been with Tessa, there wouldn't have been anything to think about. I'd have wanted things to be like this with you. You're not... *replacing* him. The two of us being together, it has nothing to do with him. Okay? You can't think anything else."

"Okay," I said, but the jab of hurt hadn't completely gone away. I believed her, and yet—it was impossible to know what would have happened then, too, wasn't it? The only way it had ever happened was that she had turned to me after losing him.

It was different with me and Tessa. I couldn't have avoided seeing that after I got back to the island, the way she closed herself off when she realized her parents hadn't made it instead of turning to me, but it wasn't as if we'd done much soul-bearing before. She was so straightforward I'd been more comfortable with her within a few months after her family moved to the island than I was with most of the kids I'd grown up with, and I'd cared about her, a lot—I *would* have been there for her, before or after, if she'd wanted it—but in that straightforwardness she'd always been clear that she didn't expect, or even want, promises about eternal devotion she wouldn't have believed we could follow through on anyway. Before I'd left for New York she'd told me that if I hit it off with someone at the academy, she'd understand, she didn't want us to force a long distance thing, so I'd said the same went for her. I'd accepted that was just how it was with us.

Kaelyn and Gav... I'd seen him look at her as if there was no one else in the entire world, to him. I'd seen how desperate she was when he got sick, how shattered when he died. It was nice to think I'd helped her put the pieces back together, but he had still been there first. He'd been a guy with a mission as big as hers, the way he'd kept the town together and organized, looking after everyone who needed it. How could he not cast a shadow?

Now, by the edge of the vast lake with the breeze tickling past us, Kaelyn teased her fingers into my hair and drew my mouth to hers, and I stopped thinking about all of that. When we were kissing, I didn't care how many shadows lingered around us. I pulled her closer for another kiss, citrus soap smell on her skin and apricot syrup taste in her mouth, and another, until I could almost believe we'd never have to stop.

Mason helped me herd all the kids except the toddlers over to the dance studio. Even at the day's brightest, the light from the front window filled only half the room. Cody, Owen, and Mya drifted toward the darker end, Cody listening as the other two muttered to each other. The rest of the kids fanned out, gaping at the space.

"First let's warm up," I said. I modeled some easy moves—touching toes, jumping jacks—and they copied me at varying paces. Then I went to turn on the boom box I'd found in a used CD shop other scavengers had left mostly untouched, along with some batteries and a few recent pop albums I thought the kids might recognize.

"I don't know how to dance," Paulette said, twisting her hands together.

"That's okay," I said. "We're not letting anyone else watch—we're just going to have fun with it. All you have to do is move with the music."

At first I had them just bounce with the beat. Then I led them from a step-touch into a simple grapevine. The little kids started tangling their feet and giggling, and even Meredith looked bored. Owen was ignoring me now, showing off some imaginary karate moves to Cody and Mya.

I'd had my first lessons more than ten years ago— and I'd *wanted* to dance, after seeing some performers at a festival in Halifax with my parents. But I didn't have to get the kids perfectly involved. All I needed was to find some way to get them putting a little of their emotions into the movement.

"Okay," I said, pausing the song. "That was just us getting used to the music. Now I want you to find your own moves. Whatever you want—it doesn't have to be 'real' dancing. You can just move in ways that show things you're feeling, maybe things you'd have trouble talking about. Like, if you're angry, you could do this." I punched my hands out at the air. "Or, if you're sad, you could move like this." I curled my back so my arms dangled, and let my body sway. "Or if you're excited, you could do this!" I whirled around. "You see?

Anything you want—there's nothing you can do that's wrong. Try things out, and if you don't like how they feel, try something else."

"This is stupid," Mya said. "Who wants to dance about *feelings*? Oh, this is my sad dance." She pulled an exaggerated pout and wiggled her arms like a monkey, and Owen cracked up.

Maybe I hadn't done the best job of explaining. But Meredith lifted her chin with that steely look and said, "*I* think it's cool, if you actually try," and the others looked at the boom box expectantly.

Mya started to sneer at Meredith, so I cut off any further complaint by saying, "If you don't want to move around, you can sit and listen to the music. That's fine too. It's been a while since we've had any."

I pressed play and returned to my spot in front of them. Meredith stepped in a slow circle, waving her arms like swooping wings. The little kids started bobbing with the rhythm again.

I should use myself as a model. What was *I* feeling? Nervous, hopeful. Letting go of any thought of technique, I twisted at my waist and reached, one way, and then the other.

"Can I go down on the floor?" Paulette asked.

"Whatever you want," I said.

She lay down and curled up, then stretched her limbs wide. A couple of the other kids sprawled on the floor nearby, squirming and rolling, though their expressions were solemn. I couldn't tell if this was helping them at all, but at least they were doing more than staring at the walls in their apartment.

"Watch this!" one of the younger kids said and did a handstand, kicking her legs in the air. I dashed over to spot her before she toppled over.

"Leo," Meredith said, "does this look good?" She raised her arms over her head in an approximation of a fifth position pose and spun on her feet.

"Don't worry about looking good," I said. "It's whether it feels good to you that matters."

A little boy tugged at my shirt, wanting to show me a stomping move he punctuated with a fierce grunt, and Paulette asked about doing leaps, and I had to catch the handstand girl before she fell off the barre after she clambered onto it. A whole five minutes might have passed without me looking around at the entire group when Meredith said, "Hey, where'd Mya and them go?"

My head jerked up. The shadowy end of the studio was empty, but there was another door there that led to the changing rooms. I walked over, expecting a prank— the three of them jumping out to startle me, probably— and found the dim rooms with their benches and clothing hooks empty. Beyond them, a short hall led to a door out the back of the building. I peered out across the small parking lot and the street, but there was no sign of the trio.

The music was still playing when I hurried back into the main room, but the other kids were all just standing, waiting. "They ran off," Paulette said flatly. "*That's* stupid."

I turned off the boom box. "I think I'd better bring you back to the condo building," I said. My heart was beating hard. I'd barely had them for half an hour, and I'd managed to lose them—some help I'd been.

"I'll look for them with you," Meredith offered, and I shook my head.

"I'll get a couple of the grown-ups. You're safer inside, Mere."

Mason was talking to Nell, Liz, and a few of the other adults in the condo building's lobby. When I told him about the missing kids, he grimaced.

"They would have," he muttered. "Those three... I shouldn't have left you to try to keep an eye on all of them by yourself. Come on."

Liz joined us, and we returned to the dance studio, checking to confirm the three weren't just hiding. Then we set off from the back entrance, splitting up across the street to peer through store windows, down alleys, over fences.

"They'll come back when they get hungry," Liz said when we regrouped at an intersection. "It's almost lunch time." But none of us seriously suggested giving up the search. Maybe we would have given them a chance to come back on their own in the world before, but now...

A high-pitched shout carried on the breeze, and I thought, *Mya*. Spinning, I jogged down the street in the direction I thought the shout had come from. A laugh followed it, and then a little shriek that could have been excitement—or pain. I ran faster.

On the far corner, movement flashed amid the skeleton of a partly-constructed house. The winter weather had darkened the new wood, and the protective plastic sheets drifted in ripped swaths like flaking skin.

Mya had climbed to the second level, which didn't have a floor, and seemed to be searching for a way up to the roof. Owen was perched in a hollow window frame below her. Cody edged along a beam nearby, arms spread as he wobbled over the open pit of the basement. My voice caught in my throat.

Cody swayed, and sat down on the beam. Mya paused, gripping one of the wall boards, as Mason came up beside me. She glanced down and spotted us.

"Oh, man," she said with a sigh.

"Get over here, you three," Mason said, planting his feet. "What do you think you're doing?"

"Having real fun," Owen said from his window. "No one's using this place. Why shouldn't we?"

"Because it's dangerous," I said. "And if you hurt

yourself, we don't even *have* a hospital to take you to."

"So what?" Mya shrugged. "Everything's dangerous. Probably we're all going to die soon anyway, right? So why can't we just do what we want?"

The words, and her indifferent tone, made my stomach twist. I glanced at Cody, and he stared back at me, chin jutting defiantly.

"I don't want to hear you talking like that," Mason said. "Let's go, all three of you, *now*. You're already in trouble, but you can be in more, you know."

Owen groaned, and the three of them scrambled to the lawn, Mya shimmying down one of the supports using the crossbeams like a giant ladder. They reached us rumpled and dirt-smudged but intact, and none of them talked the entire way back to the condo building.

But what did it matter if they weren't talking like that, if that was what they were thinking?

I knew even going in that it wasn't likely to make a difference, but I'd still asked Dorrie if I could have a few minutes alone with Cody, away from the other kids, and she'd managed to convince Owen and Mya to tag along with Mason to grab snacks for the group. So there we were, in the bedroom Cody and Owen shared, me and the boy I'd talked into leaving his home and his mom. He'd drawn his knees up onto the cot and was looking away from me with a particularly determined scowl.

"I'm sorry," I said to his profile. "It's awful—I know it's awful. My mom and dad, they both got the flu. But for you, I know it's even more awful, because you were there with her. And I asked you to leave her. And that was kind of an awful thing to do too. But it would have been even more awful to stay. It isn't your fault. It's the virus, the friendly flu, it's— Sometimes there aren't any good options. Okay? No one here thinks you did something wrong. We all just want to help you feel all right again—and Owen and Mya too, really. No matter what you've done or do, we'll still be here."

He didn't answer, didn't so much as glance toward me. I swallowed. "Look, if you want to be angry at someone, go ahead and be angry at me. I told you that you should come with us. It can be my fault. You want to yell at me? You can."

Nothing. His fingers curled into his palms against his leg, skin almost as pale as the white threads along the unhemmed edge of his cut-off shorts. His blond hair was falling into his eyes, in need of trimming. With that coloring he could have been my opposite, but we had enough in common. There had to be a way I could get through to him.

"If there's anything you'd want, from me or anyone, I'll do it," I said. "You just need to tell me. Write it down if you don't want to say it."

He turned his head toward me, studying me with those cool blue eyes.

"I don't know if you agree with what Mya was saying yesterday," I went on, "but it isn't true. We're alive, and we can stay alive, if we're smart about it. There are a lot of awful things, but there are things to stay alive *for* too. Maybe it doesn't seem that way now, but—after a while it'll get easier. I promise. And talking to people, letting them know how you feel, that helps."

He made an odd sound in his throat. For a second I thought he was working up to speak. Then he spat in my face.

"I think I handled it as well as I could," I said to Kaelyn a few hours later, as we took a minute to relax after washing a bunch of laundry in one of the rainwater collecting basins set up on the rooftop patio. I leaned against the low concrete wall, looking out over the few blocks of roofs and treetops between us and the lake. "I didn't get angry, just reminded him again that he could tell me if he wanted anything, and left. But I don't know if he really listened—maybe I just made things worse."

"I'm sure it sank in that you're trying, that you care about him," Kaelyn said, propping herself against the wall beside me. "Even if he can't accept that yet, it has to be good for him to know it."

"I guess."

She shifted closer so our arms touched. "*You* know you did the right thing, don't you? Convincing him to come with us? If we'd left him with his mother, either one of them would have managed to get her out and she'd have infected him, maybe even hurt him... or he'd have had to listen to her the whole rest of the time, through the hallucinations too. That's not something a kid should have to hear."

Her voice had gone raw. She'd listened to Gav through his entire last day, crouched against the wall beside the room we'd had to confine him in, looking ready to die herself. I turned to slide my arm around her shoulders, and she leaned into me.

"And then who knows if he'd have been able to find food, or clean water, or everything else he'd need to survive," she went on. "He'd have been all on his own."

"I know," I said, "and I'd do it the same way again if I had to. I just don't know what I can do *now*."

"You're trying your best," Kaelyn said. "I think I remember someone reminding me a little while ago that we can't save everyone."

"I think using my words against me is cheating."

She poked me with her elbow. "I'm pointing out that they were smart words. Some days I think we should consider it a huge victory that we save anyone at all."

"*You* saved all sorts of people by getting the vaccine

to the CDC," I said. "Drew said the new batch will be here soon, right?"

"Michael's just finished making arrangements with the CDC. It sounds like they're going to send that one doctor, Ed—the nice one—up here with their part of the batch. Two or three days, and then everyone here will be protected."

"From the virus, at least," I said, but I was relieved to hear it. Two or three days. We could make it that long.

"Then we can start thinking about other things," Kaelyn said. "When everyone's vaccinated, it'll be easier to start coordinating with the other people still around... There might be some things we can get up and running again. I mean, obviously some we're going to have to give up on, at least for now, but... the electricity here was hydro, it's not like Niagara Falls has gone anywhere. There've got to be people left who can figure stuff like that out, if we get more organized."

"Yeah," I said, though it was hard for me to imagine that big a future. So I settled for hugging her and thinking just a few days forward, to the vaccine and the one enormous looming fear it would wipe away. That had to change something—for Cody, for the other kids, for all of us.

* * *

The faint sense of relief lasted until the next afternoon,

when Dorrie came down to the basement where I was sorting through our most recent scavenging haul.

"Have any of the kids come by here?" she asked.

A creeping sensation tickled up my back. "No. Why?" I said, already suspecting—and dreading—the answer.

"Owen, Mya, and Cody took off again," she said. "I had to help one of the little guys in the bathroom, and when I came out they were gone. Mason's already headed over to that house where you found them last time. I'm sure they haven't gone far."

In spite of those words, her face was tight with worry. This was her whole job, looking after the kids. Whatever guilt I'd felt the other day, she'd have it ten times worse.

"I'll help look for them," I said, setting down the blanket I'd been folding. "This can wait."

Several of the adults had gathered in front of the building. As we joined them, Mason appeared, alone.

"Not at the house site," he said.

"How long have they been gone?" I asked Dorrie.

"Half an hour, maybe," she said, her mouth twisting. "I checked all through the building first—I didn't think they'd have just *left*. We've told them enough times how dangerous it could be out there."

"They're pushing their limits," Mason muttered.

I thought about what Kaelyn had said yesterday,

and what Mya had said, before. Maybe they were pushing *our* limits—seeing how far we cared, how much danger we were willing to face for them. How much their lives were really worth to us.

"Why don't we split up, so we can cover more of the neighborhood quickly," Nell suggested. "Dorrie, you could head south; they might have gone to the beach. Mason, wherever you haven't checked to the north. I'll go east and Howard can go west."

"None of us should be walking around alone," I said —we couldn't forget the city *was* dangerous for us too. "I'll go with you, Nell." Owen had been begging Mason to let him come on a scavenging expedition a few days ago. Maybe they'd gone east toward the main commercial strip on an expedition of their own.

Kaelyn and some of the others had come out to see what was happening. We broke into groups of three, Kaelyn joining Nell and me as we headed down the street, not talking, just listening. The kids were smart—I figured they'd have put at least a few blocks between us and them before they paused anywhere.

It was hard to be quiet. Glass from broken store windows crunched against the sidewalk under our shoes. We passed cafes and restaurants, clothing boutiques and art shops. I could imagine couples with arms linked and groups of laughing friends strolling once upon a time where we hurried now.

My gaze snagged on the spot where we'd come across the corpse, the memory bringing a twinge of nausea. At least the kids hadn't had to see that. We'd managed to protect them from a sliver of the full horror of what we were living through.

"Do you think we should—" Kaelyn began, and my ears caught a sound that made my body tense. I held up my hand, and she fell silent. There—a voice, too muffled to distinguish words, but definitely a voice, up ahead.

Kaelyn and Nell had obviously heard it too. We walked on as quickly as we could without drowning the voice out with our steps.

"Why are you hiding?" someone said, the question carrying through the battered door of a dress shop down the block. "We can play a game, but I don't really like hide and seek. What are your names?"

It was a girl's voice, but not Mya's. She sneezed, and Nell's face stiffened. We all reached for the strips of cloth we used as makeshift face masks.

"Get away from us!" another voice answered— Owen. With all his posturing stripped away, he simply sounded like a terrified little boy.

"Wait here," Kaelyn said to Nell. "Leo and I can get them out."

"We don't want to play with you!" Mya shouted as we edged closer to the door. Peering inside, I saw a girl who looked to be in her early teens rubbing her nose as she leaned to peek around the racks of clothes that scattered the store at odd angles like a maze. The kids must have been hiding somewhere deeper inside, cut off from the entrance.

"Hey," Kaelyn said gently, and the girl whirled around. She stared at us, her eyes widening, and then her fever-splotched face split with a grin.

"More of you! Are you all together? I was starting to think there wasn't *anyone* around here anymore."

"There's a bunch of us," Kaelyn said in the same soothing tone. She took a step back, and held out her arms beckoningly, like she would have a wounded rabbit, a frightened puppy. "You should come out here, and we can talk."

The girl looked over her shoulder, but the kids had gone quiet. She ambled toward the door, scratching her upper arm. "Did you go to Malvern?" she asked. "Maybe I've seen you around school before. So many people there, it's hard to remember."

"No," Kaelyn said, continuing to ease away, up the street in the opposite direction from Nell and me. She shot me a glance, and I nodded. "I'm not from around here, not really anyway. We can go for a walk and I'll tell you about it."

The door creaked as the girl pushed it open. She wobbled a little, but her gaze stayed trained on Kaelyn. "Where are you from then?" she asked as Kaelyn guided her farther away. "How long have you been here? I stayed home, inside, for a long time, because for a while it was looking pretty scary out here, but then, after Dad didn't come back... I *had* to see."

As soon as they were past the front of the store, I ducked inside. "Mya, Owen, Cody, let's go," I said, keeping my voice low.

Mya and Cody emerged from the curtained changing stalls by the back of the store, Owen from under a shelving unit displaying sequined sandals. "She's gone?" Mya whispered, her gaze darting past me.

"For now," I said. "Come on, quickly."

I held out my hands. Mya and Owen just rushed past, but Cody grabbed ahold of me, trembling.

"Here we go," I said to him, copying Kaelyn's reassuring tone. When I ushered him outside, Kaelyn and the sick girl had already reached the end of the block. Nell motioned for us to head back to the condo building.

"We didn't mean to—it was just, we heard someone talking, and we wanted to see who it was," Mya was explaining in a thin voice. "She didn't *sound* like a bad person. We didn't know she was sick. We went in and we couldn't see her right away, and then she got in front of the door—she was trying to *hug* us, and saying how happy she was to see us—but she was coughing and scratching..." Her mouth clamped shut, her face pale.

"We got as far away from her as we could," Owen put in, his hands clenched into fists. "She wouldn't get away from the door."

Nell looked grim. "It's good that you tried to keep your distance," she said. "We'll have to keep you apart from the other kids, the way we did with Cody when he first joined us, until we're sure you're okay. All right? I'll have Dorrie bring your favorite things so you won't get too bored."

A shudder passed from Cody's hand into mine, and a wordless sound broke from his throat. "I don't want to get sick!" he wailed, the first words I'd heard him speak since that evening when he'd been pleading with his mom.

I bent down, and he threw his arms around me, burrowing his face in my shirt. My eyes burned. I glanced at Nell over his shoulder, her expression as distressed as I felt.

"It'll be okay," I said, but I couldn't put any conviction into the words. Maybe it wouldn't be. He'd finally spoken to me, and it was to ask for one thing I had no way of giving him.

Less than twenty-four hours later, Drew turned up with a cooler holding forty doses of the vaccine. Kaelyn looked at him and bit her lip as Nell told him what had happened with the kids.

"We've got them quarantined in separate rooms," Nell said, preparing her equipment to administer the shots. "I don't think they were exposed for very long. They could easily all be fine. I'll give them their vaccinations upstairs after I've finished everyone else's."

"And if they do get sick, we can try the transfusion treatment that worked for Meredith," Kaelyn put in.

"What are you planning on doing if they get sick and that *doesn't* work?" Drew asked, with a hesitation in his voice. I wondered what the Wardens had been doing when they found out someone was infected.

"We'll keep them as comfortable as possible, and hope," Nell said, but I knew she hadn't seen a single person survive the virus who hadn't already caught the earlier, non-fatal version that had partly protected Kaelyn, Howard, and Liz, or responded well to a transfusion—which, from what I understood, had only happened a couple times after Meredith.

"And we're doing the same for the girl who exposed them," Kaelyn said. We'd managed to isolate her in a store-top apartment down the street, with some food and water.

"Well, just be careful," Drew said. "And don't use more medication than you have to on a lost cause. The city was mostly dry of sedatives and painkillers before the Wardens even started looking, and it's not as if anyone's making more."

"So what do you think we should do with 'lost causes'?" Kaelyn asked, and he averted his gaze.

"Just be careful," he repeated.

I noticed she didn't tell him what we'd learned from Anika about veterinary medications, which were what made up the largest part of Nell's dispensary at the moment. Anika. Another shadow we carried with us: the image of her fallen body, the blood on her back where a Warden had shot her…

We'd found a decent stash of pills in an animal clinic nearby, so the Wardens might not have figured that trick out for themselves yet. The other obviously valuable buildings in the neighborhood—grocery shops, corner stores, pharmacies, multi-residence buildings like this one—had been thoroughly picked over before we'd arrived. Of course, even the veterinary medications would run out eventually. Maybe it would be smarter and kinder to put a person who couldn't be cured to sleep, rather than hold out for the miniscule chance they'd survive.

I didn't think any of us here was quite ready to decide that, though.

I went with Nell when she brought the last few doses up to the quarantine condo. It had two bedrooms and a den, none of those very large, but the kids seemed to have accepted the restriction. Mya's face was drawn, but she complained about her breakfast and asked for several things from the penthouse suites as if nothing unusual was going on. Owen wanted to know whether the vaccine would stop the virus if he'd caught it, and when Nell admitted it wouldn't, started talking about how he'd hardly been near the girl. And Cody had sunk back into muteness. He stared at the floor the entire time we were in the room with him, his only response a slight wince when Nell gave him the shot.

"I'll come back and keep you company a little every day," I told him. "More, if you want."

He didn't respond, but I remembered the way he'd clung to my hand, the panic in his voice. I wasn't waiting for him to ask now.

Nell's chosen quarantine period was fourteen days, because she hadn't seen anyone infected go that long after exposure without symptoms. I spent an hour each of those days with Cody, bringing a game or a deck of cards to play with, and a book I'd read to him when— inevitably—he ignored my offers. I had no idea if it was making any difference to him at all, but it made *me* feel a sliver better, knowing he knew I'd be there. I looked in on the other two too: Owen always snapped at me that he wanted to be left alone, so after a few times I let him be, but on the second day Mya said she wouldn't mind a few games of Crazy Eights. I stopped by her room each time after Cody's. She never admitted to being worried, but she never smiled either, not even when she won.

Everything we'd accomplished—everything Kaelyn had accomplished, carrying her dad's notes and the vaccine all the way to Atlanta, arranging the compromise between the CDC's doctors and the Wardens, leading the islanders here—it hadn't been enough. Maybe nothing we did would ever be enough to keep the people we cared about out of danger. The virus could mutate again. The Wardens could revolt against Drew and slaughter us. Some other group of survivors could decide to attack our little haven without warning.

It was even more impossible to predict the future than some alternate past. All we could do was wait and see.

On my eighth visit, I'd been reading for twenty minutes when Cody got off the cot and sat down next to me. Not leaning in, not reaching out, just sitting close enough that our knees touched. My heart leapt, but I didn't make a big deal of it. I read until the end of the chapter, and when I closed the book he got up and returned to the cot. I wanted to think his shoulders were a little less slumped.

"You're more than halfway there," I said. "You made it through before; you can do it again."

On the eleventh day, I arrived just as Nell was leaving the condo. Her face was pinched, her eyes wearier than usual. I stiffened.

"Who?" I said.

She sighed. "Owen's temperature is up. Only a couple of degrees, but... he's also itching."

"And the other two?"

"Nothing concerning. But we can't know for sure yet."

"No," I agreed, a guilty relief penetrating the knot in my stomach. Owen must be terrified. He might have frustrated the heck out of me, but he didn't deserve this. But... at least it wasn't all three of them. If I'd brought Cody all this way just for him to get infected after all, I didn't know if I'd be able to forgive myself.

He still hadn't spoken, but he came to sit next to me as soon as I settled on the floor now. On the twelfth day, he rested his head against my arm. I had the urge to hug him to me, the way my mom used to when I was little and we read together, but I was afraid to push for any more. I watched him, carefully—the way he rubbed his knee, tugged at his hair—tensing until he stopped, wondering if it was beginning.

But the second week ended with a faint smile on Nell's face. I yanked open Cody's door as she let out Mya.

"You're free!" I told him. "Quarantine's over. We're sure you're not sick."

His face lit up so bright I wouldn't have been

shocked if he'd glowed in the dark. Then it fell when he stepped out and he and Mya looked at one another, registering that it was only the two of them.

"Where's Owen?" Mya demanded, her chin already quivering.

"He's in the hospital room," Nell said. "Howard's giving him a transfusion."

"You mean he's infected." Mya glared at her. "Are you going to make him better? You have to make him better!"

"We're going to do our best," Nell said, and Mya burst into tears.

"That's not good enough!" she said, covering her face. Cody stared at her, and then at me, and all at once he lunged at me with fists raised. He pummeled me with his hands as I grabbed him. I flinched when one caught me in the gut, but I didn't let go.

I'd held that other boy, months ago—grabbed him and run from the charge of that wild bear. What Cody was running from, I couldn't help him get away from. At least I could stand and suffer it with him.

After a minute, his blows softened. He gripped my shirt, tears trickling down his face, and a sob hitched out of him.

"It's not fair," he said in a small voice. "It's not fair."

"I know," I said, and oh, I did.

* * *

Cody didn't retreat into silence again, but he seemed to have decided he'd only speak to me. When I went up to the penthouses, he asked me how Owen was, whether the transfusion had cured him, and all the kids watched me while I answered.

"It'll take a few days before we know," I said, holding another fact heavy inside me. Nell hadn't noticed any improvement in Owen's symptoms so far. The girl who'd infected him was dead, her transfusion giving her just a momentary break from the fever before she'd careened off into the hallucinations that came before the virus finished its awful work.

I had to give the same answer the next day, and the next. If the kids had been lethargic before, now they looked as if they'd sunk into numbness. The older ones meandered around the condos' living areas, contemplating the toys and games and books but rarely trying any activity for even a minute. Mya and Cody sometimes refused to leave their bedrooms at all. When I'd look in on Cody, he'd be huddled with his face to the wall. I sat beside him, put my hand on his shoulder, and he didn't tell me to go away. That was as good as it got.

The gloom touched even the toddlers, who squabbled, poking and pinching at each other until Dorrie or Mason had to step in. Meredith still came with me to visit, but when I left, she did too.

"I'm sad about Owen," she said to me. "But I feel

more sad when I'm there. It's like the whole room is full of sad."

I knew what she meant. We were drowning in it.

On the fourth day after Owen's transfusion, I passed Nell in the hall on the way to breakfast, and she just shook her head. If the treatment had been going to work, I had the feeling it would have by now.

"You know what," I told Kaelyn. "I'll grab something to eat later. I'm going over to the studio for a bit."

Once there, I stood over the boom box, sorting out my thoughts. I'd encouraged the kids to dance out their feelings here just a few weeks ago, as if it were simple. It should be. There was music in sadness—how many songs had been written about loss and loneliness? I needed something to loosen the lump in my throat, the twist in my chest.

I put on an album by a particularly mournful emo band and slipped from my warm-up straight into a routine I made up as I went. I moved with the slow beat, the quavering melody, but no matter how I threw myself into it, the worry inside me didn't release. My mind kept returning to the kids in their playroom, doing anything but playing. To Owen on his bed downstairs, coughing and sneezing and probably already veering into manic chatter.

Finally I stopped, panting and damp with sweat, and crouched down beside the boom box. For a few long minutes I just hunched there, my face tipped against my knees, listening to the ragged rhythm of my breath. Then I wiped my eyes and switched off the music.

I could try to bring the kids over here again, but that hadn't seemed to work any magic before. Dancing was my thing—that didn't mean it would be theirs—and it didn't always work even for me, obviously.

Outside, the morning sun was baking the pavement, the breeze from the lake taking only a bit of the edge off the rising heat. It was one of those early June days when you'd think summer had already arrived. Seagulls squawked overhead, wheeling against the cloudless sky, and a sudden homesickness hit me, even though I knew the home I missed didn't exist as anything but a town full of ghosts now.

As I approached the condo building, my eyes caught on the form of whoever was standing guard just behind the front door. I stopped, my skin tightening at the thought of walking in there. Letting that door shut behind me, and the next, and the next. I saw in my mind all those closed doors shutting Owen away from the others, holding the kids from running away, waiting to quarantine anyone else who was exposed...

How could we not be drowning? Of course Cody and the others had wanted to run. We were smothering ourselves with fear, calling it safety, when really we were never going to be safe. Nothing had ever been totally safe, even before—not riding in a car or playing on the beach—but we'd done it anyway, because that was how you lived. You didn't wait to be pulled into some perfect world, you learned to breathe in the world you had.

I was sweating again, the sunlight searing my hair. I knew what we would do, living in this world, on a day like this.

There was a store we'd looked through briefly but dismissed as not very useful a while back that I nonetheless remembered. It wasn't *useful* I needed today. I filled one of the shopping bags still hanging behind the counter with an array of sizes and patterns, marched back to the penthouse condos, and dumped my haul in the middle of the living room floor.

"We're going swimming," I announced.

The kids stared at the heap of bathing suits. Paulette moved first, digging through them to find the few that would fit her, and the little kids scrambled over to join in. Cody took a hesitant step toward them, and then paused, wavering. Mya looked to Dorrie.

"Kaelyn said the water might not be safe," Dorrie said with a faint frown.

"The sewage system hasn't been used in months," I said lightly. "That's months for any bacteria to wash away. These guys have survived a heck of a lot—I think they can take on the tiny bit of dirt that's left so we can have a lot of fun."

"Yeah!" said one of the five year olds, with the first real grin I'd seen in days.

"Please, Dorrie," Paulette said, clutching a blue tankini. "It's so hot."

Dorrie held my gaze. I hoped she was thinking through some of what had occurred to me earlier. She sighed, and shook her head in bemusement.

"All right, no scaredy-cats here."

The little kids gave a cheer. I went to grab some of the extra towels from the storage area, to change into the swim trunks I'd found for myself, and to find Meredith. When we returned, even Mya and Cody had put on suits. Meredith pounced on a purple one with frills that I'd figured she'd like, and in a few minutes we were all tramping down to the beach. Dorrie insisted we slather ourselves with sunscreen, which I had to agree was probably smart. Then we treaded across the rough sand to the water's edge. Dorrie had brought Mason and Howard to play lifeguards, but they hung back, giving us space.

The kids picked up energy as they went. Meredith raced over to one of the fingers of boulders that protruded from the shore into the lake, and Mya and Cody darted after her. Dorrie stayed with the little kids as I followed.

"Here I come!" Meredith shouted, and leapt into the water. She emerged with a laugh, droplets gleaming in her braided hair. Mya slithered in after her, but Cody hesitated and glanced toward me.

"You want to jump together?" I suggested, offering my hand. After a moment, he smiled and took it.

"One... two..."

"Three!" he finished for me, and we sprang off the algae-slick rock into the waves.

The lake wasn't deep there—I hit the water wide to stop myself from plummeting. Cody dogpaddled around me, his smile stretching into a grin.

"Bet you can't catch me!" Mya called.

"Bet I can!" he retorted, and pushed off the rocks in pursuit.

Paulette was floating starfish-style, gazing up at the sky. Meredith dove down to the bottom and tugged on my foot. The toddlers stomped along the shoreline beside Dorrie, the other little ones wading in to their waists. They patted their hands against the surface, watching the spray of drops sparkling in the sun, and spun around with bursts of giggles. Farther back, Mason shaded his eyes as he and Howard watched.

Mya and Cody swam back toward me, Mya trying to hide behind me, Cody dodging one way and then the other. He tapped her arm.

"Got you!" he crowed.

"Climb up," I said, motioning to my shoulders. I helped Mya clamber on and propelled her off into the water.

"My turn," Cody declared, and I launched him too. He stayed under for one anxious heartbeat too long, and then came up sputtering and beaming. I forced myself to exhale slowly as he and Mya kicked toward Meredith in the shallower water. He was okay.

He looked like a real part of the group for the first time since he'd joined us.

As I trailed behind, I realized that for the last several minutes I'd forgotten why we were here. Forgotten to dwell on the home we'd left fleeing the friendly flu, on the boy lying sick back in the condo building. It looked like the kids had too. Those troubles weren't gone, but for this brief sliver of time we were just people taking joy in the water. The shadows hadn't followed us here. And it was fun that had chased them away, not guns or locked doors or solemn plans.

We were relearning how to breathe.

"Leo," Meredith said, swimming a little farther out, "can you touch the bottom here?"

"Let's find out," I said, and plunged after her.

Later, as we were walking back wrapped in our towels, Cody turned to me. "Now that I've got the vaccine, do you think I could go hang out with Owen a little?"

I opened my mouth with the instinct to discourage him, but I caught myself. Why stop him from giving his friend some comfort in what were probably Owen's last days—the way Cody hadn't been able to comfort his mom? Nell would shield him from the worst.

"That's a nice idea," I said. "He might not be... really himself—you know that, right?"

Cody nodded, with a twist of his mouth. "I just thought he must be getting really bored, on his own."

"Yeah," I said. "He probably is. When we get back, I'll tell Nell you want to see him, so she can come get you when it's a good moment."

By the time I made it back to the apartment, Meredith had already changed and run off to rejoin the other kids. "It looks like you all enjoyed yourselves," Kaelyn said.

I ran my hand over my still damp hair, sunscreen smell drifting from my skin. A sense of home, transplanted here.

"Yeah," I said. "I think it was good for them."

"*You're* good for them," she said, giving me that quietly bright smile that could melt me in an instant. It hit me, in a way it hadn't really before, that she was right.

I'd given them what no one else had thought to.

Then she lowered her gaze, looking almost embarrassed. "There was something you said, a while ago... It occurred to me that this might help." She picked up a book I hadn't noticed sitting on the kitchen island—one of her journals—and offered it to me.

"The first entry, it'll explain what it is," she said.

I opened the well-worn cover.

Sept 2

Leo,

It's about six hours since you left the island.

My fingers tensed around the journal as her voice from several months ago spoke about her regrets—not coming to see me off, letting our rift linger on that long —and her promise to be braver. When I reached the end of the entry, I glanced up at her. She was resting her hand awkwardly on the counter, a hint of a blush in her cheeks, but she looked right back at me.

I loved this girl. So much.

"Kae..."

"That isn't the important part," she said. "I just wanted you to know why I started writing first. The part I really think you should see is..." She took the journal, flipped through the creased pages to a spot she'd bookmarked with a scrap of paper, and handed it back. "When I was sick."

Oct 24

You know how people in books and movies make deathbed confessions?

I didn't want to think about Kaelyn sick, about how

close she'd come to dying—but I kept reading. And, as I absorbed the words, my dread faded.

I remembered the day she'd written about: the summer we were fourteen, the walk along the beach, the kid who'd stopped us with his pointed questions. Reaffirming that we were bound together not just by friendship but by the respective colors of our skin, as islanders but outsiders. I'd had no idea how Kaelyn had felt, though.

This time, as I stood there looking at you, it made me want to kiss you...

I wanted you to be more than my best friend.

After I'd made it back to the island from New York and seen her and realized how close I'd come to losing her, how much *I* wanted her, I'd wondered how long that feeling had been growing inside me without me noticing. Whether that was why I'd been so particularly stung by the things she'd said to me in the heat of that one argument, years ago. Somehow I'd never considered that she might have had similar feelings.

You're going to spend the rest of your life believing our friendship meant nothing to me, when really the problem was I cared too much.

"I didn't know," I said quietly when I put the journal down. Kaelyn took it, turned it in her hands, and set it down again.

"I sort of told you," she said. "When we got to

Atlanta—when we first really kissed?"

I had a vague memory of some mention of fourteen. "I think I was too caught up in the kissing part to be paying much attention to anything else," I admitted.

She laughed. "Fair enough. I guess it's been hard to talk a lot about anything that happened... before. I'm never sure how much it's going to hurt, bringing things up. For me or the person I'm talking to."

"Yeah," I said. There were so many questions I'd thought of asking her but hadn't, for the same reason. I put my arm around her, hugging her to me. "Maybe we should stop worrying about that. Maybe if we talk about it more, it'll hurt less." Casting light on the shadows. Letting go of the breaths we'd been holding.

"I'm starting to think so." She looked up at me. "So that's what I meant before, when I said us being together is just about us, not anyone else. You meant that much to me before I'd ever met Gav. What I felt, for him—it's two separate things."

In that moment, I saw all my love reflected back in the warmth of her gaze. No shadows, no blurring. Just her and me. Just *us*.

It was possible she'd never seen echoes of what might have been when she looked at me. Maybe that had been in my head too.

"Okay," I said, and this time I completely meant it. I touched her cheek, kissed her, let my head rest against hers. The room was quiet around us, but there was music here all the same, if you knew how to listen for it.

"Dance with me?" I said, without any doubt how she would answer.

She didn't speak, just set her hand in mine.

ACKNOWLEDGMENTS

There are two sets of people who deserve most of my thanks here:

To the Toronto Speculative Fiction Writers Group —specifically, Senaa Ahmed, Arvin Gupta, Lorne Kates, Stacy King, Gale Merrick, Carolyn Moore, and Siri Paulson—for offering feedback on these stories when I needed it and getting me on track where I went astray.

And to the Fallen World trilogy's readers, who stuck with me and Kaelyn all the way through our journey, and have so often send kind words and support my way. These stories literally would not exist without you.

Thank you all, immensely.

ABOUT THE AUTHOR

Like many authors, Megan Crewe finds writing about herself much more difficult than making things up. A few definite facts: she lives in Toronto, Canada, with her family and three cats (and does on occasion say "eh"); she tutors teens with special needs; and—thankfully—the worst virus she's caught so far is the garden-variety flu. She is the author of The Fallen World trilogy (*The Way We Fall*, *The Lives We Lost*, and *The Worlds We Make*) as well as *Earth & Sky* and *Give Up the Ghost*. Visit her online at www.megancrewe.com.

Made in the USA
Las Vegas, NV
17 January 2022

41426226R10121